ALL THE FIGHTING PARTS

ALL THE
FIGHTING
PARTS

HANNAH V. SAWYERR

AMULET BOOKS • NEW YORK

Cataloging-in-Publication Data has been applied for and may be obtained from the Library of Congress.

ISBN 978-1-4197-6261-1

Text copyright © 2023 Hannah V. Sawyerr
Book design by Deena Micah Fleming

Printed and bound in the U.S.A.
10 9 8 7 6 5 4 3 2 1

ABRAMS The Art of Books
195 Broadway, New York, NY 10007
abramsbooks.com

The victim who is able to articulate
the situation of the victim
has ceased to be a victim:
he or she has become a threat.

—James Baldwin

For the girls affected by the actions of
S███████ B██████████
We won.

THE MORNING I SPENT IN A POLICE STATION

remembering all that I have forced myself forgetful,
is a morning I felt smaller than a whisper.

A day I remember for my confusion,
my father's rage, and a world full of presumptions,
I began the process of making small

everything that has tried to make
a wreckage of me. In front of a county detective
and a lukewarm water, I sat

wrestling with a story the world
would rather listen to, while proclaiming a truth
that once seemed bigger than my

whole body.

Nobody tells you what it's like.

You hear about the spotlight,
the coffee-stained breath,
but nobody tells you about the stares.

Eyes so judgmental,
you have to convince yourself
you aren't the one who committed a crime.

If I remember anything about Detective Walbrook,
it'd be her adult acne, messy dyed hair,
and wrinkled uniform.

All of which I'd rather focus on
than sharing my story
while my father sits next to me.

Maybe it's the hypocrite in me.
Focusing on flaws of others
before focusing on myself.

I couldn't remember the last time I ran a comb
through my hair or slept the whole night through.

But this isn't a story about sleeping habits,
poor hygiene, or overdue hair appointments.

Although this is the first time I told the full story,
it won't be the last.

Some hear my story and feel guilt.
Others think I'm brave.
Some even think I'm lying.

If you remember my story for anything,
remember this:

*I am a warrior on the days I shout
and on the days when silence wraps me
in its arms like my only friend.*

Sometimes I feel my worth is determined by how loudly I riot.
As if surviving is not enough.

But if you listen closely, even silence carries a story worth telling.

Katie Walbrook: Hi, Amina. My name is Detective Walbrook. I spoke with your father earlier and it's my understanding you would both prefer he stay in the interview room with you?

Amina Conteh: Actually I—

Nigel Conteh: That's right, I'll be staying.

Katie Walbrook: All right. Amina, I'll start by saying I understand this is a difficult time and I want you to know this is very brave of you.

Amina Conteh: Uh-huh.

Katie Walbrook: If at any time you need a break, let me know and we can take a short pause.

Amina Conteh: Mhm.

Katie Walbrook: Please answer verbally. Stay away from nods or "mhm" or "uh-huh" so we are all clear for the transcripts.

Amina Conteh: Uh-h—I mean okay.

Katie Walbrook: Let's start with the basics. I'm going get to know you a bit. How old are you?

Amina Conteh: I am sixteen years old.

Katie Walbrook: Where do you live?

Amina Conteh: 102 Fuller Road. In the city.

Katie Walbrook: And how long have you been there?

Amina Conteh: My whole life—

Nigel Conteh: For about thirteen years. We moved there when Amina was three.

Katie Walbrook: Thank you. Okay, and where do you go to school?

Amina Conteh: Springfield.

Katie Walbrook: So, that would make you a junior at Springfield High School, correct?

Amina Conteh: Yes.

Katie Walbrook: Thank you.

AUGUST 22:
4 MONTHS BEFORE THE ASSAULT

PRESIDENT GROVER CLEVELAND

Grover Cleveland was the only president to serve two nonconsecutive terms.

That is the answer to Ms. Hamilton's question.

Based on the three wrong answers she's received,
the crickets you can hear in the room,
and the frustration you can read on her face,
I know she is begging for someone to provide the answer.

My hand remains unraised,
the way it usually does,
hiding under my desk with my phone—
texting Talia:

Amina: Milkshakes after school?

Yesterday, I got a "firm warning" from Ms. Hamilton
when my phone rang in class.
She threatened to call my dad,
I promised it wouldn't happen again—

but I never promised I'd be off my phone.

TALIA, AND OUR FRIENDSHIP

Talia and I have been friends for longer than any presidential term.
Even longer than Grover's nonconsecutive-serving ass,
and this is the first year we aren't sharing a class together.

Talia and I have always had each other's backs.

When I almost got suspended for skipping class with Deon,
Talia told our teacher I was in the bathroom with cramps,
turning my possible suspension into a firm
"Don't let it happen again."

When Talia almost flunked out of history last year,
I saved her by writing her final (A) paper.
Bringing her potential (D) average
to a solid B-.

Talia: It's the least you can do, honors kid!

Leaving me in a class with your clown of a boyfriend Deon

and that Holly girl from your church.

You know she's raised her hand like five times already???

SPRINGFIELD HIGH SCHOOL

Springfield is the only high school in this part of Baltimore,
and until two years ago,
the school *nobody* wanted to send their kids to.

After receiving a city grant for technology and athletics
all those kids from Franklin High—
a white school *everybody* wants to send their kids to—

marched their way to our school's main office
with parents wagging transfer papers in the air.
All of a sudden,

our school wasn't too hood for their kid anymore.
Now at Springfield High,
you may experience a bit more racial tension,

and you'll *definitely* hear a lot more Taylor Swift.

Amina: Someone's mad they still can't talk to their crush

As for Holly, she been like that since I've known her

And I'm not an "honors kid"

HISTORY WITH HAMILTON

Knowing your history
is as important as feeding your body,
or knowing your language.
I don't hate history.

I hate the *class* that is *Honors* History.

Especially Honors History with *Ms. Hamilton*.

It doesn't help that her outfits reek of boredom—
her most exciting accessories are her kitten heels
and stiff-ass pearls draped around her neck
(probably gifted by her fourth husband).

Not only did I have to switch out of the only class
Talia and Deon and I would have shared together,
I am also one of only five people of color here
and the *only* Black girl.

My classmates are allowed to not have the answers.
Meanwhile, they *expect* me not to,
and sometimes I get tired of proving when I do.
And even worse—

dealing with the stares when I don't.

Talia: Fine, you got me on the crush thing.

But you? Not an honors kid? Please.

NOT AN HONORS KID

There is a difference between
being a student who takes an honors class
and being an honors student.

I've never been an honors student.

While the other kids marched into class
on the first day with backpacks loaded with
three-ring binders, highlighters, and an unlimited
supply of different colored pens,

I sat with the same notebook I bought for every class,
accompanied by a pencil borrowed in first period
and never returned.

The principal's office is a room you'll find me in
almost as often as you'll find an honors student in a library,
always for the dumbest reasons.

Like the time a teacher caught me walking across the street
to buy myself a sandwich because,
damn, sometimes a girl is tired of cafeteria meat.

Or the time I got caught writing history essays for money
after a dumbass told one too many people, but
shit, why not make a profit from the gifts God gave me?

And most recently, for disrespecting Ms. Hamilton.
Why lie when instead of teaching history, she should be teaching
"How to Lull a Class to Sleep" instead?

A subject that used to be my favorite
is now a one-hour block of proving my worth,
by choosing between
rising above the standard or
sitting through the assumption I can't.

CAUGHT

Grover Cleveland was the only president to serve two nonconsecutive terms.

That is what I say after Ms. Hamilton calls on me without warning,
slipping my phone away while I answer.

"We've moved on from that. If you focused on class
instead of your phone, you would have known."

I apologize, zip my phone away in my bag,
give Ms. Hamilton the attention she's crying about.

BOWL CUT

A boy who isn't even worth naming decides to talk shit.
I call him

"Bowl Cut,"

because he's been rocking the same tired-ass
bowl-shaped haircut since preschool.

Bowl Cut whispers in a not-so-quiet way,
letting the whole room know he wants to be heard:

"Do they let anyone in these classes now?"

CAGED BIRD

Anyone walking in my shoes
would understand why Bowl Cut, Wannabe History Wiz,
should have shut his not-so-smart-ass mouth.

Anyone would understand why I respond by saying:

"You don't have to act out because your mom's
been giving you the same tired-ass haircut since pre-K, Bowl Cut."

Anyone in my position would understand
why Bowl Cut should've quit while he was ahead.

Instead he says:

"I think Amina is grappling with the idea
that she doesn't have to take everything so personally."

Anyone would understand why I respond by throwing a highlighter
I probably borrowed from him
while words flew right out of my mouth
like I am a caged bird, but instead of learning how to sing

I learned how to holler:

"I think this asshole is *g r a p p l i n g*

                with the fact that I DON'T GIVE A FUCK!"

SOMETIMES I ACT . . . BEFORE I THINK

"Foul language and disrespect will not be tolerated,"

Ms. Hamilton says after Bowl Cut gets a highlighter
to his head, the way he deserved.

All Bowl Cut does is force a goofy smile
to protect his little ego—
acting like the side of his head don't hurt
where my highlighter hit him.

Ms. Hamilton continues to speak on presidential elections
and trivia nobody in this honors class knows,
strolls to my desk with her little sticky notes pad,
slaps a pink sticky note on my desk
with her little manicured pink nails:

Expect a phone call home today.
—Ms. Hamilton

Shit.

BACK TO (HISTORY) BUSINESS

Hamilton returns to the front of the room,
occasionally ungluing her eyes from the board
to make sure my phone stays away.

When the bell rings, I pack my things,
leaving the note on my desk right where Hamilton left it.
Text Talia:

Amina: We might have to rethink those milkshakes.

PHONE CALLS WITH PASTOR JOHNSON

I come home to what I think is an empty apartment
only to find my father already home from work.
This time it's not because his boss let him go early
after a slow day of answering calls at the dental office.

With a scrunched frown on his face,
a Bible on the counter,
and a phone to his ear,
my father says the words I've heard time and time again:

"I need this child to listen!"

No use in telling him just how much Bowl Cut had it coming.
Always getting his nose in *my* business
because *he* has no life outside of school.
My father says,

"Pastor Johnson and I've decided you will help around the church.
Like that one nice girl, Holly, who goes to your school.
For tonight, go to your room and write your teacher an apology."

Not only did my father compare me to Springfield High's angel
and Holy Tabernacle's sweetheart, Holy Holly,
but I also have no proper defenses.

Yes.
I *did* tell Bowl Cut I don't give a fuck.

But I can't tell my dad how Bowl Cut messes with me
when I don't know an answer.
He would only say,

You should have known the answer in the first place!

I can't tell him how everyone in class laughs
because I'm the butt of his corny-ass jokes.
He would only say,

You shouldn't care what your little peers say!

All he cares about is his daughter not talking back,
because to him, talking back is no better than throwing punches.

My foot does not land on the third step of the staircase
before my father ends his phone call.
I prepare myself for the next words I know he will say.

This is when he says:

"You inherited all the fighting parts of your mother."

MOTHER

My mother was a woman who knew her
rage was as powerful as her love.

In the first grade when a teacher told me a boy was
"only teasing me" after he kicked me in the shins during recess,
my mother marched right into the principal's office the very next day.

I don't remember what my father had to say,
but I do remember my mom making every adult in the room fearful
for even *thinking* of allowing someone to disrespect her daughter.

My mother passed later that year.

On these days, I wish she was here even more.

MOTHER (2)

My mother spent her days
extinguishing flames she did not ignite.

A sought-out doctor in Sierra Leone,
but told her license was invalid in the States.

As if immigrants have foreign textbooks and foreign bodies.

A healer,
saving lives while risking her own.

A rebel,
defiant when the world told her not to be.

My father worries women like us always get burned.

There's an old proverb:

"Even a fool is thought wise if he can keep quiet.
So a woman is safe if she can mind her own business."

Or however it goes.

HER REFLECTION

It is true I am my mother's mirror—
kinky curls misbehave like hers,
skin deep in color like hers.
My words,
my weapon,
sharper than any blade.
Just like hers.

My father thinks I have too much mouth for my small frame.
Always says,

You inherited all the fighting parts of your mother.

APOLOGY LETTER DRAFT #1

Dear ~~Ms. Hamilton,~~

~~Sorry I acted out because Bowl Cut decided to be a bitch.~~

APOLOGY LETTER DRAFT #2

Dear Ms. Hamilton,

Thanks for that phone call home. You really gave my father AND MY PASTOR something to chat about. All during the first week too. Impressive. Maybe you should learn how to handle your own class instead of getting my father involved? ☺

APOLOGY LETTER (FINAL)

Dear Ms. Hamilton,

I am writing this letter because I understand I behaved inappropriately. The behavior I exhibited today is not true to my character, and you deserve to teach in an environment where you and your students are respected.

I understand disrespect will not be tolerated. I should not have used the foul language I used in your class and I certainly should not have thrown a highlighter.

I apologize for disrespecting you, and I look forward to the rest of the school year in your class.

Sincerely,

Amina C.

JIGSAW PUZZLE

My family and I used to spend Friday nights
hunched over a coffee table
crafting a showpiece also known as a jigsaw puzzle.

The only item other than her own glasses and coasters
my mother ever allowed to make a home
of her good dining room table.

Thanks to Pastor Johnson
I have more time than ever
to practice them again.

GOD-GIVEN BLESSED TYPE OF LUCK

If you are lucky enough—
I mean, God-given blessed-type lucky—
you may find

                                        a hidden gem

chillin' for purchase at a yard sale.

The kind that collects dust unopened
until a rainy Saturday morning demands furniture

                                        be pushed out of its way

as it sprawls across the coffee table.

We gathered for days until their completion.
Sitting
                        crisscross
applesauce
while we searched for the right fit.

My puzzle tonight finds a home across my desk,
still has that smell-of-wet-cardboard
even-when-completely-dry,

                                found-at-the-back-of-a-yard-sale charm.

EXPECT THE UNEXPECTED

Puzzling is an interest most don't expect
from a high schooler infamous for always having a rebuttal.

Last year, my vice principal suggested
I join Ms. Hamilton's debate team
because of all the "energy" I carry.
His way of saying *shut your ass up* during classes.

I made it through two months before being kicked off for
behavioral reasons—
in other words, Ms. Hamilton learned I told a boy to *fuck off*
after he commented on my 'fro,
didn't even give me a chance to explain,
and still kicked me off the team.

Fast-forward to this current school year,
and Ms. Hamilton is the only teacher teaching Honors History.

So now she and I are *both* stuck with each other.

SURE, I LIKED DEBATE

I was good at it, and it gave me something to do.
But I'd rather practice patience while creating something
than defending something.

What people don't know about debate
is that it requires more patience than a fire tongue.

Patience to learn what your opponent is saying,
to learn just what to say to sway an audience.

Sure, I'm forced to spend a Friday night in the house
but it's not like Talia and I confirmed plans.

Even though Deon's mom works night shifts
and he and I wanted to chill at his place tonight,
the way my father will be watching me like a hawk,
I can't link with him either.

Besides, they wouldn't be down to puzzle anyway.

THE NEXT DAY

on my way out to school,
I tuck the letter I wrote Ms. Hamilton at the bottom of my bag.

As I enter her classroom in the morning,
she looks at me,
smug smile on her face.

"I trust after speaking with your father yesterday,
we won't have any problems today, right, Amina?"

I nod.

Smiling at Ms. Hamilton,
I reach for the bottom of my bag,
rip the letter, and toss it into the trash.

What Ms. Hamilton doesn't know won't hurt her—
she doesn't have to know I wrote her a letter.

What my father doesn't know can't hurt him—
he doesn't have to know I didn't give it to her.

As far as Pastor Johnson is concerned?
This isn't his concern to begin with.

Besides,

I wasn't fucking sorry anyway.

POLICE INTERVIEW TRANSCRIPT:
AMINA CONTEH
JANUARY 24
09:39 A.M.

Katie Walbrook: Can you tell me about your relationship with your church, Holy Tabernacle?

Amina Conteh: That's not my church anymore. I believe you mean my prior church, Holy Tabernacle.

Katie Walbrook: Yes, my apologies, Amina. When did you originally join the church?

Amina Conteh: I'm not sure. Maybe ten years ago?

Nigel Conteh: Yes, that's right. Ten years and this is how they treat us.

Katie Walbrook: When you did attend, would you consider yourself active members of Holy Tabernacle?

Amina Conteh: Yes, I don't really remember because I was young but I think the only time we've ever taken a break was after my mom—

Nigel Conteh: Yes, we were active.

Katie Walbrook: Thank you.

SEPTEMBER 14:
3 MONTHS BEFORE THE ASSAULT

SAME OLD SUNDAY MORNINGS

No matter how many colds I fake,
in my home, Sunday mornings are always the same.

Unless you have a 102-degree fever,
or are puking through your nose uncontrollably,
from 9:00 a.m. to 2:00 p.m. your ass is in a church pew.

I'm not sure if I've ever truly liked church,
but for my father,
the church is a place of refuge.
A safe place to rest in.
And if you've attended as many services as I have,
the church finds a way to become a part of you.

You hate the man who always tells you
You've grown so much!
but can never remember how to pronounce your name.

You hate the woman who says your dress is
Soooooooo cute!
and would be
Soooooooooooooo much cuter!
if it could be just
a little longer
or
a little looser.

You hate all these things,
but love the old woman
who has been there your entire life—
and most of her own too—
who smiles at you
from the same (unofficially) assigned church pew
occasionally offering you bottom-of-the-purse candy
(the best kind of candy).

You fall in love with the drums accompanying the organ
while that one woman shouts "Glory!" at the top of her lungs,
starting what I like to call

a
　　　holy
　　　　　ghost
　　　　　　　domino
　　　　　　　　　effect,
also known as a church-wide "praise break."

It becomes worth it when I see
my father—a man whose face
remains soldier stone straight—smile
whenever Pastor Johnson shares an encouraging word.

It becomes worth it on the days
when I can remember my mother only in
fragments.
I remember,
this is a place that made her feel whole.

SAME OLD SUNDAY MORNINGS (AT HOLY TABERNACLE)

If you're a pastor who is loved as much as Pastor Johnson,
you have entire congregations paying 10 percent of their salary
to support the church's light bill—and a church-approved BMW.

My father and I used to sit in the third row from the pulpit,
but if the first two weren't reserved for elders and ministers,
we would probably be seated so close to Pastor Johnson
he would spit on us every time he yells.

About a year ago, my father accepted the fact that
I don't want to sit near enough to the pastor to smell his B.O.,
and he lets me hide in the back pews now.
Although it may have more to do with having to sit next to a daughter
he nudged awake every thirty minutes.

I'll never be the saved & sanctified daughter he prayed for,
like the daughter of Holy Tabernacle's most involved family,
Ms. Holy-Roller Holly Robertson.
Present at every church function,
every Wednesday and Friday night Bible study,
volunteering at every Sunday afternoon bake sale.

AFTER TWENTY MINUTES

of hiding in the bathroom on my phone,
I sneak into service late,
sink into my same spot in the same back pew.

A woman sits next to me,
hands folded in prayer,
but I hear what sounds like snoring.

Usually, I can make it through service only if I bring my journal.
When I was younger, I journaled because my mom did.
She always said,

"Everybody has a story to tell and a song to sing."

She would share memories from her childhood and her village.
Stories about being the only daughter in a family of six men.
Stories about speaking against injustices in her community.

I DON'T HAVE MANY STORIES

& I wouldn't put anyone through the torture of hearing
my vocally challenged ass sing even a hypothetical song.

But during the moments when
I don't want to be here—and wish
my mom *was* here—my journal makes the two-
(or three-) (or four-) hour service worthwhile.

Most people assume I'm using it for notes,
but usually, it's just to talk shit about Pastor Johnson's suits.
So big, they look like his daddy passed them down to him,

and his daddy probably did.

A PEACE I CANNOT PROVIDE

Pastor Johnson started preaching at Holy Tabernacle
after his father retired,
and because he's a few years younger than most pastors,
he's slightly easier to listen to.

His sermons are only barely shorter than his father's
and his jokes are barely better too,
but as corny as he can be
he offers a space for people,
like my father,
to feel at peace.

Truth is,
Pastor Johnson and his church give my dad a peace
I may never be able to provide.

DEON'S TONIGHT?

As soon as I sit in the pew,
my phone lights up with a text from Deon:

Deon: My mom might be working late tonight.

Since we'll both be at my uncle's event,

you wanna get together tonight instead of next week?

Deon's mom isn't nearly as religious as my dad.
Shit, he and his mom attend Sunday services only on Easter.
But occasionally, he says something about his "uncle"
that reminds me I'm dating my pastor's nephew.

Deon and I have gotten pretty good at sneaking around,
partially because Pastor Johnson has known Deon since birth.

September 14

After getting in trouble with Ms. Hamilton, my father and Pastor Johnson decided "the right thing" for me to do is volunteer at tonight's Unity Cookout, but do you even get holy points for volunteering for shit you don't want to? Doesn't that take the "good deeds" part out of it if I don't even want to be there?

The only positive thing to come from this is the fact that Pastor Johnson has been raving about his "talented young nephew" for so long he actually convinced Deon to come. But outside of Deon, it's not like I'll actually enjoy the event like everyone else. We were supposed to have sex next week, but maybe because his mom won't be home after the cookout that will happen sooner rather than later?

THE UNITY COOKOUT

At church, we "Praise Him in Advance" for every "Brighter Day"
to the music of artists like Marvin Sapp and Kirk Franklin.

At school, you ain't nobody if you're listening to
anything outside of the *Billboard* Hot 100,
and if you're gonna listen to any gospel,
it better not be anything other than the ghetto gospel that is
Juvenile's "Back That Azz Up."

The Unity Cookout is a fusion of both my worlds.

Holy Tabernacle, along with local organizations in the city,
sponsors it at the beginning of every school year.
They invite the whole community for good music,
a good time, and even better food.

It's the only time of year you'll find old church folk dancing
to "Wobble" (with a too little much wobble for wobble's sake),
as opposed to lifting their hands to praise and worship.
It's the only time church ladies wear short shorts
rather than the below-the-knee skirts they wear every Sunday.

Old folks teach us music by playing the classics.
It's where young folks like me
first learned about the magic that is the music by
Stevie Wonder and Diana Ross.

And if we're lucky (and most times we are),
the old folks let us teach them our legends too,
like Cardi and Bey.

We don't always agree on song preference,
but we can all agree
a plate of fried fish by Mr. Walker
smothered in Ms. Weaber's homemade hot sauce
with a side of Mr. Redd's mac and cheese
followed by any and every dessert
coming from Ms. Brown's oven,
can heal any wound.

Bringing out more of our similarities than differences.

Ain't nobody ever complain about a good time—
and even better food.

LONG-ASS CHURCH SERVICES

After service ends an hour late,
Talia hits me up:

> **Talia:** Soooooooo, can I come with you to that cookout??

> I overheard Julia say her family's store is a partial sponsor.

> All of a sudden I think it's bout time I bring my agnostic behind to Jesus!!!

Her Julia-obsessed self.
Figures Talia wants to come because she'll be there.

My father barely lets me leave my room these days,
and the only time Talia has been allowed over
was to "study" (bullshit) for a "test" (nonexistent) we had the next day.

But if I know one thing, it's that my dad would never say no
to me bringing a friend to anything associated with Holy Tabernacle.

During the ride my father listens to his favorite gospel tracks
and hums along to every song

I ask if Talia can come over before the cookout and catch a ride.
He barely even thinks about it.
I already knew his answer would be:

Yes.

FASHIONABLE FRIENDS LIKE TALIA

A fashion-forward friend might ask to pick your outfit for a cookout,
but fashion-forward friends like Talia ask to pick your entire outfit—
including your panties.

Best friends like Talia say:

"You need underwear that *flaunts* your ass! Not covers it!"

Talia says:

"If you see Deon tonight and you're in the moment
and you start feeling the conversation,
and you start feeling each other,
you'll be happy he's not feeling on your six-pack Walmart panties."

Says I'll be thankful she didn't allow me to wear
underwear the size of a flag marking my uncharted territory.
I tell her,

"Deon said his mom *might* be working late tonight."

Besides, just because Deon and I haven't had sex,
doesn't mean he hasn't seen me in my underwear.

I remind Talia I'm not volunteering at any party.
It's an annual block party,
with every family,
a.k.a. every adult,
a.k.a. every parent in our community.
Sponsored by a *literal church*.

But Talia only says:

"Okay, but is it *in* a church?"

PERFECT PANTIES

Talia's family has the money for her to believe
the solution to every dilemma is an entirely new outfit.
Says,

"You know if we had a little bit more time,
I could have driven us to the mall to get you some new clothes—
and some *real* underwear."

Sometimes she offers to buy things with her allowance.
Her intentions are always good,
but it's hard feeling like you're taking some sort of handout.

Even when I refuse, she just
gives   gives   gives

I don't want to be the friend who can only
take   take   take

So, I always pretend I don't want it.

"Girl, not everybody is as obsessed with clothes or *panties* as you are!"

It's hard knowing as much as I'd *like* to dress the way she does
I never can because *I ain't got the cash* the way she does.

JEALOUS (I'M NOT SUPPOSED TO BE)

I know you're not supposed to be jealous of a friend
and I know it's worse when you're jealous of a best friend,
but at times I wish I could trade lives with Talia.

Talia is tall and thin and can work any outfit she owns.
She never has to worry about a bad hair day.
Her hair falls down her back after being straightened
every two weeks by the Dominican Hair Gods at her aunt's salon.

Talia has both her parents at home,
and both of them would rock the whole world
if anybody tried to hurt her.

Don't get me wrong.
I know how to walk into a room,
be the loudest person without speaking.

Hips that occupy the space of a small doorway—
I may not be stopping traffic,
but I'm known to make a guy
do a not-so-quick double take.

Deep brown skin that can steal a sold-out show,
the sun serves me as a personal bronzer.

Hair that shrinks in water,
and a self-esteem that grows with my ability
to speak up and call out anyone's bullshit.

But sometimes it feels like as much as I love the way I look,
I live in a world that doesn't.

While Talia lives in a world that does.

SEXY . . . ADJACENT.

After rummaging through my clothes,
probably looking for a thong she'll never find, Talia figures
my red romper, faux leather sandals & a plain black pair of panties
are *sexy adjacent* and will do.

Says I'm "lucky" she doesn't cut the cheeks out.
That most guys would
"like them better if I would just cut the damn cheeks out!"

I agree to wear the plain black flag panties
(with both cheeks intact),
raising a white flag in surrender.

BALTIMORE.

Fact One: For the past few years, the Unity Cookout
has been held on the sunniest day of September.

Fact Two: I am unsure if God exists, but if he does,
this sunny day is proof he's looking out for my city.

Baltimore.

It may be hard to fall in love with my city's grit,
given the news reports you may see,

the murders and the poverty they report,
but it's impossible to not fall in love with my city's charm.

This year, local stores have partnered up
and have snow cones and school supplies to give away.

A line of people stretches to the end of the block for boxes
of free groceries sponsored by local orgs for those in need.

As much as I would love to have news stations
lining up to report this part of who we are, they won't.

This is the part of Baltimore people outside of the city never see.
The part of the city—that stays in the city—for only us to know.

I'M ONLY HERE FOR THE FOOD . . .

Pastor Johnson and my father have me serving food today.
But if I have to be forced to volunteer for an event,
by the food is exactly where I want to be.

All my favorites are there:

Mr. Walker's fried fish,
Ms. Weaber's homemade hot sauce,
Mr. Redd's mac and cheese,
and Ms. Brown baked a cheesecake
my mouth's already watering for.

Talia insists I sneak away and
go over to Deon to request a song so he can see my outfit,
but nervousness rushes over my body,
and it's like my feet won't allow me to move.

... AND DEON.

It's not that I don't *want* to see him—
the boy looks good.
Fresh haircut,
glowing brown skin,
sneakers on point,
with the world's brightest smile.

Deon is the only guy who has ever made me nervous,
all in the best possible ways.
We've been together for three months now—technically.
Depending on how you define the word *relationship*.

It was something fun at first.
Something with no titles.
We hooked up a few times,
and we never actually went *all* the way,
but I still found myself falling for him.

He didn't go around telling all our business,
bragging to all his friends like a lot of guys at my school do.
He's kind.
Sweeter than the guys I've been with before.

What originally started as two people texting
turned into me always checking on him after a bad day,
which turned into him always surprising me with my favorite snacks,
which eventually turned into us hooking up less
and going on dates more.

I don't know what it is about nice guys.
Until Deon, if a guy ever overwhelmed me,
I would talk to him less and less
until I eventually didn't talk to him at all.

But I can never manage to do that with Deon for too long.

That's the thing about relationships.
Deon proved sometimes you can't always see them coming.

It's never too long before I see something that reminds me of him,
or I find a photo to send him because I know he'll laugh,
or he'll smile real wide with all his teeth—
and I'm roped right back in like a fish out of water,

and Deon is the only guy who owns a fishing pole.

ONE CONDITION

"I overheard Deon talking to his boys about you.
Real mushy and shit. Trust me, he really likes you."

This is a benefit of having a friend who's in everybody's business
but her own. She *always* got ears in the right places.

Lately Deon's been saying I've been distant as if I like him *less,*
when really, I talk to him less because I like him *more.*

She nudges me to go talk to him.

"Your pastor won't notice if you leave for a second.
Besides, I didn't pick out your clothes for nothing."

I agree. On one condition.

"If I go talk to Deon, you need to go find Julia."

I point in Julia's direction.

Talia offers her hand and we shake on it.

Deal.

AWKWARDNESS IS EXPECTED.

But if there's one thing I know about Deon,
he won't let me feel that way for long.

I request a song and in a matter of seconds
it's blaring through the speakers.
I apologize for being out of touch;
he smiles at me,
wide enough to show that gap in his teeth I love.
Says,

"We should move on to more important things.
Like how nice you look today."

Thank God for best friends who meddle, because
thanks to Talia's fashionable eye, I do.

Before I can bring up plans for tonight,
Pastor Johnson walks in to ask how Deon is holding up.

DEON'S DAD

Deon and Pastor Johnson are so comfortable with each other,
you would think Pastor Johnson was Deon's dad.

Deon's dad is alive—but that's pretty much
all Deon knows about him (other than the fact that he lives
across the country and calls twice a year).

Pastor Johnson has always been someone Deon looked up to
& while Deon's mom and brother don't live in the church
the way my father does,
knowing that Pastor Johnson means so much to Deon
is enough to make him at least *all right* in my book.

MINA?

After a few minutes of conversation, while they both pretend
I no longer exist, Pastor Johnson looks at me and says,

"Mina! You know you're supposed to help serve the food.
I want to give your father a good report for today!"

I don't know why he's calling me "Mina,"—
only people who I am close to call me that—
but I smile anyway.

Pastor Johnson may not mean any harm,
but he is one of those people that gets
too comfortable
too quick.

Pastor Johnson continues talking to Deon,

"Hey, Deon, I'm not sure what this song is
but kids are having a little too much fun if you know what I mean."

He's the only one who laughs when he says it.
He continues,

"Think you can play 'Revolution' by Kirk Franklin?
And Mina, let's get back to work to make this a successful event!"

There he goes with that Mina shit again.

HOLY GHOST TRANCE

Deon changes the song and looks at me in a way that says,
I have no choice but to follow the boss's orders.

Immediately, everyone starts shouting and flinging their arms
as if they are under some sort of Holy Ghost trance.

My father is clapping along with the music,
Holy-Rolling Holly is rocking back and forth
with that "Christlike joy" she rambles about.

I can even see a cheekless-underwear-wearing Talia
fumbling with her hands while speaking to a smiling,
curly hair–flipping Julia.

REVOLUTION.

It ain't all bad.
Honestly.
Watching all these people
lifting their hands,
shouting "Glory, Hallelujah!"
praising a God they can't even see,
reminds me of how a church
actually *does* mimic a revolution.

On its best days, the church mirrors a people protesting

the lifting of hands   mirrors the raising of fists
shouting in a church aisle   mirrors shouting in the streets

all for a change only a revolutionary can see.

No matter where they grew up,
where they come from,
the people of a church and the people of a revolution
share one thing:

They believe in *something,*

and that motivates me
on the days when I can't manage
to believe in anything.

THREE HUNDRED DOLLARS

"So what's it like DJing for your pastor uncle?"

I say after Pastor Johnson finally leaves.
Deon says it's an easy gig,
that he loves to play music he knows makes people feel good.

"He mentioned he's always looking for people for different jobs.
If you wanted to work for him, I'm sure he'll look out.
He's paying me three hundred dollars for today."

Three hundred dollars for a day's work doesn't sound all that bad.
And if I work for him enough times,
I could finally dress and look the way I want to,
instead of looking and dressing only in ways I can afford.

PLANS FOILED

Pastor Johnson walks by and Deon yells:

"Yo! I talked to Mina about how I got this job through you;
maybe you have a job for her too?"

To my surprise, Pastor Johnson barely pauses before he responds,

"You read my mind!
I was actually going to ask Mina if she wanted a job.
If you do well today, I certainly have one in your future!"

Pastor Johnson gives me his card and a wink before walking away.
Deon looks at me and says,

"Now let's talk about tonight.
Turns out my mom might be home after all.
Plan for another time?"

He gives me a quick kiss on the cheek and tells me to get going.

Just like that.
I may not be able to spend tonight with Deon,
but I can't complain about being offered a job.

Pastor Johnson might not be that bad after all.

Katie Walbrook: Are you familiar with a young lady named Holly Robertson?

Amina Conteh: You mean Holy-Rolling Holly Robertson? Who isn't? The whole church knows her. They love her because she's such a goody-goody.

Nigel Conteh: Amina, be respectful.

Katie Walbrook: Can you tell me about your experience with Holly? What exactly was her relationship with Holy Tabernacle?

NOVEMBER 1:
1½ MONTHS BEFORE THE ASSAULT

WEDNESDAY NIGHT BIBLE STUDIES

A TV evangelist's voice blares through the living room speakers:

If you want to be saved, call the toll-free telephone number
on your screen for just a low fee of ninety-nine cents per minute!

It's time for Wednesday night Bible study.

I brush my teeth and get dressed,
playing my own music through my headphones—
I know better than to play it out loud before a service.

As we leave and get in the car,
my father plays the same old gospel CD:

Singers of Praise: LIVE!

I only touch the stereo if I want to hear my father say
I only listen to "secular music"
in a "secular world" and soon,
I'll be doing those "secular things."

HOLY HOLLY

The first thing I see as I enter the church
is a Fall Harvest donation table run by Holy Holly.

She's been a member of Holy Tabernacle
since before she could breathe.
Her parents have been members since before they could too.

My normally stingy father gives her money without question.
He doesn't even ask where the money goes,
despite questioning me every time I ask for more than two dollars.

Holy Holly thanks us.
Says,

"God Bless!"

She breaks down her table before service starts.
Everyone, including my father, runs to her rescue.

"Don't you worry about that!"
"Go on head inside, we got this!"

MAYBE I LOOK FRIENDLIER THAN I AM

Maybe my father's donation of his money
convinced Holly I was willing to donate my ear.

Because when I walk into the church, she trails right behind.
Starts asking me all these questions:

Hi! It's a lovely evening, isn't it?

What's new in your life?

How is it we both attend this church, but we barely speak?

As if a reason doesn't exist for that.
I tell her I'm fine and ask her how she's been.

Big mistake.

HOLY HOLLY NEEDS NO INVITATION

Holy Holly might be the only person on the planet
who *actually* answers honestly when asked about their day.

"My brother Jonathan is dealing with a lot right now.
Pastor Johnson has been helping. So that's good I think."

She asks me if she can have a seat next to me.
I want to say I prefer to sit alone,
but she's already found a seat—right next to mine.

My eyes glance at my phone,

Deon: How about this Friday?

HOLY HOLLY WITH HER HOLY HANDS

All it takes is one strike of the organ for Holy Holly
to throw her head back and wave her Holy Hands in the air,
praising and worshipping as if she's competing
with every resident old head in the building.

I have a seat and ignore the stares, because at my church,
whoever *isn't* undergoing an exorcism is in the minority.

Amina: Friday is perfect.

November 1

All this waiting and rescheduling Deon and I are doing has me wondering whether we should have just did it in his brother's car that night. With Deon, I wouldn't care if we did it in a car, his house, or even behind a stairwell. (All suggestions I've made before.)

But Deon says he wants the first time to be special. I wonder about that sometimes. What makes sex "special"? It'll be special no matter what. Because he's special. And he thinks I am too.

If it were up to me, I would call Deon, sneak out of service, and we would do it right here, right now, in the church basement.

Okay, maybe not in the church basement, but behind a bush down the block or something.

HOLY TABERNACLE'S FUNDRAISING SWEETHEART

After about thirty minutes the music fades,
Pastor Johnson strolls to the pulpit, looking ready for a show.
Before he preaches,
he calls up Holy Holly to speak about her fundraiser.

Times like this I understand why people
say church folk just want your money.

She walks to the pulpit and begins to talk about her goal.

"I plan on distributing one hundred care packages for those in need!"

The whole sanctuary roars with applause.

I'm not cruel—
I know the importance of helping others.
After my mom passed, my father and I struggled too.
I know the importance of giving what you can.

Holly gets praise for doing everything we should be doing anyway,
for doing all the things we would *all* be willing to do,
if our whole lives were figured out by present parents like hers.

Holly is modest. Saying a million thank-yous
with a smile plastered on her face I couldn't remove
with a medical-grade scalpel.

She walks back to the pew and, when she sits,
does something I never imagined she would do.

NOT SO HOLY

Is Holly on her phone?
During a Sunday service?
Holy Holly?

The snooping skills I've learned from Talia
are finally good for something.

From the corner of my eye
I can see she sent a text:

Holly: Pastor Johnson is so extra sometimes, I hate him for it.

At least he's helping our family right?

HATING ON BALTIMORE'S MOTHER TERESA

Honestly, it's about time Holly acts less than holy.

But of all the people to hate,
why would Holly hate on Pastor Johnson?
He's one of the only people in our community who gives back,
always donating his time, *and* dollars.
He's annoying, sure. But even I can admit
hating on Johnson is like hating on Baltimore's Mother Teresa.

Holy Holly must see I read her message,
because she immediately turns her phone screen off
and stares at me in a way I'd think is the Christian version of
If looks could maim.
Minus the maim part, obviously.

Guess I'm not as good of a snoop as I thought.

JANUARY 24
09:59 A.M.

Katie Walbrook: Are you in a relationship?

Amina Conteh: What does that even matter?

Katie Walbrook: Well, the truth is, it shouldn't. I'm asking because this information often comes up in these cases and I need us to discuss these things before the defense does.

Nigel Conteh: Be respectful, Amina. Detective, she is not in a relationship.

Amina Conteh: The answer to the question isn't anyone's business.

Katie Walbrook: I understand this can be hard on anyone. Mr. Conteh, would you mind if Amina and I continued privately? Usually answering these questions can be a lot for teenagers.

NOVEMBER 18:
1 MONTH BEFORE THE ASSAULT

I'VE KISSED A LOT OF FROGS

In the sixth grade there was Greg,
but he broke up with me over a (true) rumor that I kissed Chris.

In the seventh grade there was Anthony,
but I broke up with him because he always cut my lip with his braces.

In the eighth grade there was Mike—
after our unspoken breakup, we haven't spoken since.

I rode solo during my ninth-grade year
but still made out with James, Malik, David, and Alex.

I met Deon at a party the spring of tenth grade.

He may not be the first guy I've dated,
but he is the first guy who calls to ask if I've gotten home safely
or sends me sweet text messages after a long day.
I wasn't really used to that.
To the type of love someone gives you
when they want more than your body.

I'd be lying if I said I didn't spend half my day
thinking about how good he makes me feel.

Something about knowing someone you love will hold you,
and let you hold them too.

FAST

I know what people think about girls like me.
Grown folks would call me "fast."

The first time I made out with a guy,
I had a million and one questions—but after?
I didn't really have to think about it.
I didn't really *want* to think about it.
With Deon, I thought he'd let me do just that.

Not think.

But Deon is the first guy who makes me want to be better,
because when you meet someone like him,
you want to give up your pride.

Even when you swore to yourself you never would.

STUDY SESSION

I read in an article in *Seventeen*
that one girl prepared for her first time
by watching porn.

The night before Deon and I have sex,
I prepare by texting to check he has protection,
zipping the extra condoms I bought in my bag,
and getting ready for a rated-X show.

I've watched porn before,
but this time is different.
I'm not just watching—
I'm *studying*.

I lock my room door,
plug in my headphones,
and discover what the internet
has to offer.

In the first video,
something isn't adding up.
From what I've heard,
it's usually over in ten minutes.
So I'm not sure why
this one is fifty-eight minutes

long.

TWO MINUTES

is how long I let the video play
before they begin twisting their bodies
like Wetzel's Pretzels.

A woman holds her legs behind
her head like a professional acrobat,
a man holds her body
in the air like a prized soccer trophy.

They warp their bodies
into shapes I've never imagined,
making faces
I never want to see.

I try another.

This one is shorter,
and the people almost look
like they love each other.

My body warms,
the way it does
when Deon touches me.

My fingers move,
down.
Imagine how he will fit,
snug,
inside of me.

BRIGHT, RED & LACY

Talia comes over with a red sweater dress,
a gold chain, and a pair of black booties in hand.
I offer to treat her to milkshakes
since I'm working for Pastor Johnson next week.
She says:

"You don't owe me anything besides details about tonight.
I can't believe you're having your first time before me.
I never thought it would be like this!"

Talia chuckles before she reaches in her purse,
pulls out a small pink bag from Victoria's Secret.

"I have one last thing."

I take the bag and look inside—
a bright red lace thong.

TALIA'S SUGGESTION

"Now, Mina, this is only a *suggestion* . . .
but you should listen to my panty advice."

Talia argues like she's presenting
a research paper on the power of pretty panties.
I thank her. But tell her tonight I want to be comfortable—
and a lacy thong is far from that.
I laugh. Say,

"You know, Talia. You're my best friend—
but you and your panty obsession
get on my fucking nerves!"

LIES TALIA AND I HAVE TOLD MY FATHER WHEN I MET UP WITH DEON:

- Talia and I are at the library to study for exams.

- Talia and I are at her house for a movie marathon.

- Talia and I are at the mall to shop for new outfits.

Tonight's lie:

- Talia and I will be at The Shack.

The truth:

- I will be at The Shack—but not with Talia.

- Deon's mom won't be home until late tonight.

TONIGHT'S THE NIGHT

Deon picks me up around six
and we head to The Shack to grab a bite to eat.
Or maybe "fuel" is a better word for it.

That is how I convince myself to eat on a nervous stomach.
While Deon has no problem inhaling an entire burger
with every topping imaginable, I'm struggling to finish my fries.

"So my uncle said I did so well at that cookout,
he wants me to work for some Christmas program for kids.
You'll be there too, right?"

Deon continues to devour his burger.
I continue pushing my fries around my plate.
Say,

"Yeah, I'll be there.
You know Pastor Johnson used to really annoy me
but he is honestly a pretty nice guy."

Deon notices I've barely eaten,
looks up and says:

"Everything all right?"

I am so nervous my stomach may fall out my own ass.
I say:

"Sure."

DURING THE DRIVE HOME

I stare out the window counting the yellow cars we pass.

Three.

Deon fiddles with the music,
plays a Baltimore club mix station,
a hip-hop station,
a rock station,
and he finally settles on R&B.

Real subtle.

MY GODDAMN PANTIES

We've spent a half an hour cuddling,
and I can't stop thinking about how I wish I'd listened to Talia
and upgraded my goddamn drawers.

It's not like they're covered in unicorns or dog paws,
but is being the girl who is remembered
for the pineapples printed on her panties any better?

Deon asks:

"Are you still comfortable with tonight?"

I nod.

I'M READY . . .?

Do people care about underwear while they're having sex?
It's not like your underwear makes much of a difference anyway.
Should they even matter?

I take my pineapple-printed panties off myself.
Quickly.

I throw them across the room.
Even quicker.

Deon pauses.

"You know, Mina, you said you were fine,
but if at any time you're not,
you know you can let me know right?"

I nod,
kissing him
before he gets the chance to speak again.

I THINK . . .?

But then I remember the fries I ate during dinner.

I wonder,
Does my breath taste like Old Bay?
Is that even a bad thing?
Isn't Old Bay delicious?

I think,
Why am I concerned with having breath that tastes like Old Bay,
when he should be concerned about the taste of that burger he devoured?
Is it appropriate to ask for a mutual mouthwash break?

He stops.

"Maybe tonight's not the night.
I think this may be what a nervous Mina looks like.
You good?"

I GUESS NOT

There I was.
With my bare ass on this boy's bedsheets.
Unable to mask my own nerves.
Being asked if I'm *good*.

As I reach for my clothes & conjure an excuse to go home
Deon says,

"Wait, we don't have to do anything.
I want to spend time with you."

SECRETS

Tonight, I learned Deon and I love Star Wars, cuddling, and games.

We played Connect Four five times.
Loser shared a secret about themselves.
His idea not mine.
I won three times, and he won two.
I learned:

- Deon lived in six different states before moving here at twelve.

- Deon's older sister began his boy band obsession at eight.

- Deon is deathly afraid of pigeons.

Deon learned:

- I went through a poufy dress phase as a kid.

- I never learned how to whistle.

I even gave him a bonus fact:

- I have been puzzling since I was four.

OUR FLOWERS

Deon's family keeps a couple puzzles in their house
but he's never been able to complete them.
I offer to help.

After a few minutes I can tell what his issue is:

He doesn't organize.

Sort pieces by color in their own piles,
edge pieces in another,
uniquely shaped pieces in the last.
Dedicating twenty minutes in the very beginning
can save you hours in the long run.

After we've sorted,
it takes us only one hour to finish.

The final photo?
A field of yellow roses.
I like to think they symbolize a future
yet to come.

SIGNS

There are so many signs you're supposed to look for when it's not right.

Do you feel safe when you're around them?
Are they thoughtful and kind?
Do you trust each other?

But nobody tells you how to prepare when it is right.
When someone meets all the requirements.

Deon.

He's patient.
He's gentle.
He asks questions
and waits for the answer.

So what's a girl supposed to do when a guy checks all the *right* boxes?

I'M READY

I want to find out.

So, I kiss his lips,
feel the parts of his body I want to know differently,
a little bit better tonight.

Unzip my pants, he unzips his.

He asks:

"Are you sure you want to do this?"

The parts of each other's bodies,
we've both known only partially,
wholly exposed. Ready to press against.

My answer:

"Yes."

READY TO TURN THE PAGE

Deon cannot dance to save his life,
but he has a certain rhythm when he holds me.
He tells me *you are so beautiful.*

His hands, holding my hips,
like an anchor. Grounded. Pulling me close.
I tell him *I could live here forever.*

People say all these things about the first time.
That you're opening a new door.
That you're entering a new chapter.

I don't know if that's true.
But I do know, with Deon,

I am ready to turn the page.

QUICKER THAN EXPECTED

About five minutes pass when Deon says:

"That ended a lot quicker than I wanted.
My bad . . . but don't worry."

He smiles.
Moves downward,
begins to use his mouth.

DEON SAYS:

"There are other ways."

Katie Walbrook: I'm going to ask you some harder
questions, okay?

Amina Conteh: Mhm . . . I mean yes.

Katie Walbrook: Thank you for responding verbally.
Amina, how do you know Randall Johnson?

Amina Conteh: He was pastor of the church and hosts a
lot of community events in the city and I worked for
him and he promised me he would pay me and at the time
I really wanted the money and he would always be really
nice to me and speak with his pastor voice and one day
he—

Katie Walbrook: I'm sorry, do you mind slowing down?

DECEMBER 6:
2 WEEKS BEFORE THE ASSAULT

RANDALL

The first thing I learned while working for Pastor Johnson
is he hates being called "Pastor Johnson."

Says that name is for his daddy and asks
younger folk to call him by his first name,
"Randall."

Swear he would wear Jordan's on the damn pulpit
if his congregation wouldn't protest,
and by "congregation" I mean *rich donors*
and by "protest" I mean *keep their donations.*

Pastor Johnson or
"Randall"
is one of those wannabe hip pastors
who believes Christian rap is the way to get kids off the streets.

But he's also someone who people call when in need,
and even though he convinced my dad
to make me write that stupid letter to Ms. Hamilton,
he at least *tries* to connect with young people.

He once made the second Sunday of every month
"Casual Sunday," but the old heads weren't having it
and the younger crowd didn't care too much either way.
So, he traded his jeans and sneakers
for suits and dress shoes,
looking,
preaching,
sweating through his suit—just like his pastor daddy.

Because pastors,
no matter how young they are,
all have the same old soul.

EASY MONEY

The first paid event I'm working for Pastor Johnson
is a Christmas-themed game night down at the community center.
All I have to do is watch some fourth graders
run around a gym for two hours.

Easy money.

My dad drops me off at the event, no questions asked.
He's just happy I'm not on the street
under some boy, and by some boy,
I mean Deon.

After he saw Deon walk me home the other day,
he's always hitting me with questions like

"Who was that boy?"
"Where did you meet him?"
"Who are his parents?"

I was going to tell the truth,
but if the possibility of me being with Deon
has him wanting to play 21 Questions,

I'll hold off on the truth for now.
For my father's sake.

PASTORS ARE ALWAYS IN THAT LOVING MOOD

When I walk into the center,
Pastor Johnson is barking orders.

"I told everyone decorations should be hung near the entrance!"
"Has anyone checked the streaming of the movie? Come on now!"
"Someone confirm the pizza delivery! Y'all wanna be paid, right?"

In the middle of the chaos,
Pastor Johnson sees me by the entrance,
sets down his craft supplies before hugging me.

I'm not a hugger, but pastors are always in that loving mood.
I guess it has something to do with the love of God or whatever.

"You know, Mina, I've been wanting to add more jokes
to my sermons, something to get the saints laughing!
Tell me what you think of this one."

As annoying as he is on Sunday mornings,
outside of church he's a *little* funny.
He jokes,

"Which of Santa's reindeer has bad manners?"

Maybe Pastor Johnson isn't the funniest man alive,
but he always tries to make people smile.

"Which reindeer, Pastor Johnson?"

And that much I can appreciate.
Even if his jokes do need work.

"Glad you asked! Rude-Alph!"

MENTAL NOTES

Pastor Johnson assures me
since it's my first day,
I can sit out and take "mental notes"
on how everything works.

Holy Holly is here,
but she isn't doing much of anything either.
Matter of fact, we're the only two people in the room
not working.

We're also the only women in the room.

I know church culture well enough
to know what's happening here.
Church folk always want the women quiet.
To stay in their place.

But if a fool wants to underestimate me,
& I get to do less work for the same pay,
why would I complain?

Pastor Johnson just made my money that much easier to earn.

IT'S NOT LIKE WE'RE *IN* A CHURCH, RIGHT?

Deon is here and he smiles when he sees me.
I walk over to him to offer my help.
He jokes,

"Wanting to help when you don't even have to?
You must really like me or something."
I shoot back,

"My bad! I actually saw you struggling to lift those boxes
and decided to put you out your misery.
What's your name again?"

People always say sex changes things,
and maybe that's true.
But with Deon, things changed in the best possible way.
We laugh more.
Sometimes when we speak,
I find myself remembering the last time he held me,
and my body heats thinking of the next.

I shouldn't think about him this way at a church-sponsored event,
but Talia said it best:

It's not like we're *in* a church, right?

PASTOR JOHNSON CHECKS IN

When Pastor Johnson sees me offer to help Deon,
he rushes over and pulls me aside.

"Everything all right over here?
Mina, you know I said you can sit this one out."

Pastor Johnson has the world's worst possible timing,
asking if I'm okay as soon as he sees me talking to Deon.
When I tell Pastor Johnson I wanted to help,
he says:

"All right now, but you know, if at any time you want to sit out,
both you and Holly are free to do so while the fellas handle the work."

CHARITY BASKETBALL GAME

Volunteering at a church event isn't too bad with your boyfriend there.

We may not be making out in the middle of the room,
but he does make a night of hearing kids scream—
and rescuing the occasional clumsy kid—more bearable.

Toward the end of the event,
I call my father to come pick me up
but Pastor Johnson says,

"There's no need for that! Your father works hard enough.
Tell Mr. Conteh I'll drop you off on my way home."

Pastor Johnson can be a pain sometimes,
but he means well.
I say,

"Thanks, but my father is actually already on his way."

Pastor Johnson looks at me and says,

"That reminds me, we're having a charity basketball game
at your school next week. I can speak to your father
and have you sign up! Paid of course."

LOOKING OUT

When I walk to my father's car,
Pastor Johnson follows.

"Hey, Mr. Conteh, young Mina did such a great job today.
We're sponsoring a charity game the Friday before Christmas,
and if Mina is willing, I'm sure I can scrape some cash together to pay."

My father looks at me,
giving Pastor Johnson his nod of approval.

"Well, I agreed to wait at the office for a late delivery that evening.
I'm unsure if I would be able to pick her up."
Pastor Johnson says,

"Don't you worry, Mr. Conteh!
I'd be happy to take her home.
What do you say, Mina?"

Pastor Johnson may be annoying at times,
and he may tell jokes only he laughs at,
but he always looks out.

"Thanks, Pastor Johnson.
I can definitely help with the event!"
He laughs and says,

"I already told you, Mina,
call me Randall."

POLICE INTERVIEW TRANSCRIPT:
AMINA CONTEH
JANUARY 24
10:15 A.M.

Katie Walbrook: So would you consider yourself an employee of Randall Johnson's?

Amina Conteh: I guess so. I never really thought of it that way because he was my pastor. It was just an easy way to earn money.

Katie Walbrook: Can you tell me a bit about what happened during the last event that you worked for Pastor Johnson?

DECEMBER 19:
6 HOURS BEFORE THE ASSAULT

AFTER SCHOOL, PASTOR JOHNSON TEXTS ME:

Pastor Johnson: Hey, Mina!

So excited for the Hoopers for Change event at your school tonight!

I have some paperwork that needs sorting through at the church.

Can we stop by for thirty minutes before I drop you off?

I can throw in another $50.

The name of the event may not be too impressive,
but him paying me fifty dollars more is.

One hundred and fifty dollars
for only two and a half hours of work.

Amina: Hi Pastor Johnson I'll be there!

I might even be there one hour early if he needs me to be.
Shit, for the right amount I might throw the event myself.

CALL ME "RANDALL"

With one hundred and fifty dollars,
I can afford to buy myself a whole new outfit—
even down to my shoes.

With one hundred and fifty dollars,
I can afford to get my nails done—
fresh mani with a pedi to match.

With one hundred and fifty dollars,
I can afford to go to Talia's aunt's salon—
instead of wearing my hair in the same 'fro I've worn for years.

Pastor Johnson: I already told you, Mina. Call me Randall! ☺

HOLY HOLLY AND HER QUESTIONS

Holy Holly is also working.
As expected, she comes with her questions.

Do you like watching basketball?
Do you like working here so far?
How much is Randall paying you?

Yuck.
I still haven't gotten used to calling him Randall.

I shrug. If Pastor Johnson—
I mean Randall—
didn't offer her any extra cash,
there's no use in letting her know I'm being paid more.

Pastor Johnson convinced Deon to play for the game,
and while he is one of the worst players on the team,
he *still* looks good.

Like *really good.*

Even with sweat soaking through his T-shirt,
he is still one of the finest guys in the room.
Or maybe *because* sweat is soaking through his T-shirt
he is one of the finest guys in the room.

AFTER THE GAME

Deon offers to walk me home
but Pastor Johnson cuts in mid-sentence:

"Hey, mind if we head out? We still have to stop by the church
and I don't want to bring you home too late.
Besides, I'm not giving you young kids a reason to be fresh!"

He smirks when he says the last part,
but he's the only amused person in the room.

I give Deon a hug and promise I'll call when I get in.

As nice as he can be,
and as big as his heart is,
it looks like *Randall* still needs to work on minding his business.

DURING THE DRIVE HOME

Pastor Johnson says,

"I'm so thankful you could help on such late notice.
Those papers, they always build up in the office."

I tell him it's not a problem.
I should be thanking *him* for practically throwing money away.
I say:

"Yeah, Pastor, it's so awful to be paid extra
to sort through some paperwork.
What an inconvenience."

He laughs. Says:

"You're a real special one, Mina.
And I told you,
call me Randall."

SOMETHING DOESN'T FEEL RIGHT

I've been to nighttime church services before.
They run exactly the same as daytime services.
Same praise and worship set,
same offering collection,
same too-long sermon.

Tonight, there is something eerie about a church
without a congregation inside.
Something strange about being able to hear the wind from outside
because no music is playing and no people are stomping.

I ask Pastor Johnson—I mean Randall—
what needs sorting and he points to a small pile of papers on the desk.

As I sort through them,
I wonder,

Why would he need help with such a small pile?

A hand rests on my back.

"I'm so thankful for you, Mina."

My shoulders tighten
while my throat closes before I find the words I need.

I know church folk are touchy, but this feels *wrong*.

POLICE INTERVIEW TRANSCRIPT:
AMINA CONTEH
JANUARY 24
10:18 A.M.

Amina Conteh: I think I need a break now. Can we speak about something else please?

Katie Walbrook: You're doing great, Amina. Let's talk about who you've spoken to after that night in the church, but before coming here. Did you tell any friends about what happened before reporting today?

Amina Conteh: Just my best friend, Talia.

Katie Walbrook: When did you tell her about what happened?

Amina Conteh: Just a few days ago.

Katie Walbrook: Can you tell me a little bit about your friendship with her?

Amina Conteh: I guess so.

JANUARY 12:
3½ WEEKS AFTER THE ASSAULT

BROKEN SPIRIT

that night at the church   my spirit broke inside

all the quiet parts of me   a m p l i f i e d

preacher made a mess of my body   the silencing of my voice

as the world carried on   the worship music played

the offering still collected   he preaches every Sunday

on his tired-ass pulpit   delivers the word of the Lord

on that damned pulpit.

THE SHACK

"Damn, Mina, what's been going on with you?"

Talia asks when Mr. Richard delivers our shakes.

The Shack   the only restaurant in my neighborhood with
                     a working jukebox.

Walls graced   by pictures of musical legends like

Marvin Gaye   Whitney Houston   Aretha Franklin

The cash register   graced by   *Holy Holly*

who while wearing the same uniform as the rest of the staff,
still manages to spread the

Holy Tabernacle Love-of-the-Lord™

with her damn "Ask Me About Jesus" pin.

HOLY HOLLY HOLLY ROBERTSON

Whenever we step into   The Shack,
we place our orders like everybody else,
but everyone knows if Mr. Richard is there
he always takes care of us—

everyone except Holy Holly.

I pick a table closest to the window;
she comes rushing over   grin stretching   from ear to ear.

"Amina! I haven't seen you since our Christmas event!
We've missed you so much! What can I get for you?"

MR. RICHARD TO THE RESCUE

"Y'all behaving yourself in your classes?"

Mr. Richard asks before telling Holly he'll take our order.

Talia and I used to go to The Shack almost every day after school,
and since Mr. Richard owns the place,
he used to look out with a free milkshake from time to time.

But after failing my first exam this semester,
my father's been   watching
my every move, and I can never leave my house for long.

I force a smile, avoiding Mr. Richard's question.

I've learned that what people don't know can't hurt them,
and you won't catch me lying to Mr. Richard.

Talia does the talking.

"We'll have those Sinful Cinnamon shakes please."

JULIA'S WORLD AND WE'RE JUST LIVING IN IT

"I wake up thirty minutes early to do my makeup
all for Julia to STILL not notice me!"

Whenever Talia comes close to her crush,
she gets quieter than a church mouse.

I roll my eyes and sip my shake,
letting the same
                    Julia-riddled tune play.

GROWN-ASS MEN (PART 1)

At the other side of The Shack sits a group of four men,
who own about ten more years of age than Talia and me.

They whistle at us,
hollering about our tits and ass.
Mr. Richard yells at them,
snapping his faithful dishrag.

Tells them:

> "Take that shit out my shack!"

but these men are more relentless than stubborn stove grease.

GROWN-ASS MEN (PART 2)

They lower their voices but not their gaze.

Staring at Talia and me like they have no home training.

Usually when this happens,
I respond with the stankest of stank faces
or with the clapbacks
I circle around my head like,

This is why your girl left your ashy ass!

> *The world would have been better
> off if you were swallowed!*

The devil could use men like you in hell!

This time, it's as if my voice has been muted
and my stomach turns green-pack-skittle sour.

The moment when I finally respond,
I mouth the words:

> *Thank you.*

SNOOPER'S GON' SNOOP

Why didn't you give those guys the stank face I know?

Are things at home between
you and your dad bad?

Are the two of you still not getting along?

I hit Talia with a

Don't worry about it.

for every question until she asks:

"Did something happen
that you're not telling me about?"

TEARS WERE SHED

I once

heard if you

roll your eyes back

far enough, you can stop

yourself from crying. I tried &

tears fell anyway. Talia will only say

you need to tell your dad. She doesn't

know what it's like, living in a home

where the only music that plays

is a song of silence.

TEARS WERE SHED (AGAIN)

Talia hasn't seen me cry since the first grade
when I tripped over my shoelaces during lunch
and everyone in our grade laughed   except her.

Back then she said,
Don't worry about everyone else,
that *they were all stupid anyway.*

Words can't heal every wound

but she tries anyway.
Keeps saying
"I'm sorry   I'm sorry   I'm sorry."
But words can't wipe away another man's sins.

She says,
"You know you can talk to me about anything?"

I say nothing at all.
Because I know I *can*
and I also know   I *won't.*

THE LONGEST RIDE HOME

Talia sits with me.

The same way she did in first grade.

Sits with me
during the entire drive.

Sits with me
until I finish crying.

Sits with me
until we finally reach

home.

I HAVE NO LANGUAGE

When the car finally stops
Talia asks a question my tongue
has no language for.

"Are you sure you're okay?"

The lie *yes* catches in my throat.

She says,

"I know something is wrong.
You have to talk to someone."

I nod.

Tell her,

I'll think about it.

I THOUGHT ABOUT IT

during the entire drive **(H)**ome.
           as I l**(e)**ft Talia's car.

when **(I)** came home to my father **(s)**itting in the living room,
           with a cup of **(G)**reen tea face b**(u)**ried in a Bible.

about the we**(i)**ght of holding a secret under my tongue.
           about how heavy the weight would be if I spoke

I thought of everything I wou**(l)**d rather do
           than **(t)**ell an**(y)**one about what happened to me.

I think I'll keep this to myself.

Katie Walbrook: Can you tell me a little bit more about what exactly led you to report this incident?

Amina Conteh: What is that supposed to even mean?

Katie Walbrook: My apologies, Amina. Would it help if I rephrased the question?

Amina Conteh: I just don't understand why it matters if I'm here.

Katie Walbrook: I know this is difficult, but we just need these facts for the record. What led you to pressing charges?

JANUARY 21:
1 MONTH AFTER THE ASSAULT

ONCE A BITCH, ALWAYS A BITCH.

A whole semester into the school year   doesn't matter how pissed I am

        I can always count on Ms. Hamilton to act the same.

In class, Ms. Hamilton calls on me   to see if I'm still paying attention.

        I'm not.

Lately the stares have been more frequent
like a red flag waved because I'm *not t*alking

        as if anyone missed when I was.

How is it I say less in class   but people still have more to say?

As if I came back from winter break
        & everyone can tell something happened to me.

I've heard kids in my class asking in whispers: *What's her problem?*

Everything was fine when they whispered,   everything was fine

        until today.

        Bowl Cut decided to say some shit
        OUT LOUD.

WHAT I SAID WAS

I told Ms. Hamilton:

*I don't know the answer to
your stupid question.*

She kept it moving.

She's learned by now, there's
no point

in forcing me to do anything.

Bowl Cut should have taken
better notes.

Bowl Cut whispers:

She's a little angry today.

I AM ANGRY.

Because
people
share
unasked-for
opinions.

Because
I
hate
Holy
Tabernacle's
favorite
man
and
everyone
loves
him.

Because
I
don't
want
to
be
angry,
but
it's
all
I
know.

WALK OUT

Maybe something in me changed.   Maybe I am *more* than angry.

Still, while Bowl Cut has everything to say,   I only have tears to shed.

I pack my things,   walk out the room

          before anyone has the chance to see.

PRACTICE MY EXCUSES

I already know it's Ms. Hamilton's style
to call my father.
During the car ride home with Talia,
we practice all my excuses:

> *It's that time of the month.*
> *You know what I'm referring to, right?*
>
> *I really needed to use the restroom;*
> *it was an E-MERGENCY!*

We finally settle on:

> I got sick after eating the school lunch
> and needed to vomit!

"SO, WHY DID YOU WALK OUT OF CLASS TODAY?"

I tell Talia,

"I was just annoyed."

She rolls her eyes,
doesn't buy a word I try to sell.

Says,

"I'm just worried about you."

I want to tell her the truth.

I'm not okay.

I watch my abuser preach on pulpits,
& I still have to maintain a decent GPA.

Every day I shrink
smaller than my silence.
I tell her,

"Just drop it."

Talia badgers, but she knows how to take a hint.

She drops it—

TALIA DROPS IT

for exactly five minutes,

before she asks,

"Did something happen?"

I say,

"Something like what?"

Talia asks,

"Something else at school?

"Between you and your dad?"

"At your chur—"

I search for words

but am unable to control my tears

and suddenly, I can't control my mouth

and tell her what happened last month.

FEELING LIKE DAVID

Talia says she'll be *here for me no matter what*.
That it *doesn't matter how highly people think of him*.

There's a story in the Bible they teach you when you're a kid.

David and Goliath.

David was a small dude, who, with only a slingshot
and a couple of rocks, took out Goliath, a nine-foot-tall giant.

Pastor Johnson is the only beast I have ever encountered.

And underdogs only win in the stories.

This is real life.

Underdogs don't win here.

MY OWN MEGAPHONE

My
father
is
the
tallest
man
I
know
with the world's quietest voice,
I
rarely
hear.

He once said after moving to the States,
a woman spit   at him
after he asked for directions.
Still, he keeps his own words
            concealed.

I learned to be my own megaphone
after my mother passed
and for once,
it's not loud enough.

Talia says,
"Mina, you have to know people will support you."

I want to believe her—but I don't.

A WALL OF PROTECTION

Some girls get a wall of protection shielding them from this world.

Other girls   must learn   to protect themselves.

I
know
where
I
fall.

MS. HAMILTON CALLS (AGAIN)

When I walk through the front door,
my father says Ms. Hamilton has already called.

Not only did she tell him I walked out of class today,
but she also told him I failed a second exam.

He says,
"Maybe it's time you volunteered at the church again."

I want to tell my father,
I'll make up the grade.
I'll stay in the entire weekend and do all the work.

> But the words never come.

In the middle of my silent pleading,
my father answers a phone call:

"Well, actually, that is a great idea, Pastor Johnson.
Amina will be there at 6:00 p.m. sharp."

My father hangs up.
Says, not only will I be staying
in this entire weekend,
but Pastor Johnson says

he wants to speak with me tonight.

NO CHOICE

I try to convince him I have too much homework.
That if I go to church tonight,
I'll be up the whole night trying to finish.

The truth is,

if I have to be around Pastor Johnson,
I'll be up the whole night with nightmares
again.

All he says is,

"I suppose you need to start your schoolwork now.
You will be at church tonight."

WEDNESDAY NIGHT BIBLE STUDY

always looks the same in my church.
On any given week you can guarantee
Pastor Johnson will be:

- stomping his feet so hard people walking past the church can hear

- preaching for thirty minutes longer than he is supposed to

- wiping his sweaty face with the same tattered rag

I'm not sure how much he washes it—
he probably has someone washing it for him.

Pastors have entire congregations of people
worshipping the ground they walk on,
they probably have people lined up
to worship the rags they sweat on too.

THAT KIND OF CHURCHGOER

A certain kind of churchgoer regularly attends Bible studies.

This is the crowd who
never misses a baptism,
always donates during the fundraisers,
always bakes for the annual bake sales.

The crowd who
eats,
breathes,
and lives
church.

For the perfect saints, like Holy Holly and her family—
but even they are nowhere to be found tonight.

When I walk into the building,
Pastor Johnson is the first person who speaks to me.

"It's been a while since I've seen Miss Mina!"

He continues in whispers:

> *Listen, we had a huge misunderstanding.*
> *Maybe I'll call your father*
> *and instead of coming to Bible studies,*
> *we can work out paid opportunities instead?*
> *I'll throw in extra to make up for last time.*

He pretends last month was no big deal.

Flaunting around his money.
Still faking with that lighthearted persona everyone loves,
waving   and smiling at everyone who passes by.

As if he isn't the reason I haven't been able to sleep at night.
As if what he did isn't the reason I'm pulling Fs
in the only class I've never received less than an A– in.

I carry on like I didn't hear a word,
knowing he won't make a scene with his followers around,
walk straight to my same seat
in the back of the church.

He carries on,
accepts hugs and praise
from an entire congregation
ready to cling to his every word.

Carries on
like only one of our lives changed forever.

                    Maybe only one of our lives did.

BIBLE STUDY BEGINS LATE

but that's to be expected in a church like mine.

6:05 p.m.

Starting the service late is just a simple part of the routine

     6:13 p.m.

     To pass the time, grown folk chat—

6:17 p.m.

and those chats often turn into gossip—
depending on how long the conversation lingers

     6:21 p.m.

     The kids play hide-and-seek in the
     church pews

     6:24 p.m.

     stopping whenever an adult tells them to—

     6:29 p.m.

     starting all over again
     when they turn their backs

6:32 p.m.

The worship music plays, every minute louder than the last

     6:36 p.m.

     and soon, it's as if time barely even exists

6:38 P.M.

A man yells so loud,
his single voice   fills an entire sanctuary

"MY GOD!"

Our oldest member
wears a look on her face
as if she's seen a Holy

                                Ghost.

Our assistant pastor
takes the pulpit

Half the congregation has crowded   in the parking lot,

while the other half speaks
        in loud whispers to one another.

Our assistant pastor speaks,

Good evening,
ladies and gentlemen of the church

But I can't help but keep my eyes
glued on the window—

where a cop car is parked
& our city's most beloved pastor   is cramped in the back seat

THE NOISE

Children Crying Elders Praying Teenagers **Whispering**
Children **Crying** Elders Praying **Teenagers** Whispering
Children Crying **Elders** **Praying** Teenagers Whispering
Children Crying **Elders** **Praying** Teenagers Whispering
Children **Crying** Elders Praying **Teenagers** Whispering
Children Crying Elders Praying Teenagers **Whispering**

Our assistant pastor's voice isn't loud enough to speak over the noise.

Children Crying Elders Praying Teenagers **Whispering**
Children **Crying** Elders Praying **Teenagers** Whispering
Children Crying **Elders** **Praying** Teenagers Whispering
Children Crying **Elders** **Praying** Teenagers Whispering
Children **Crying** Elders Praying **Teenagers** Whispering
Children Crying Elders Praying Teenagers **Whispering**

EVERYTHING OUR ASSISTANT PASTOR SAYS

goes through one ear and straight out the other

I spoke with Pastor Johnson   *it is his request this be handled*
quietly   *and we carry on with service.*
You may have noticed   *he is not resisting*
arrest, and he promises   *this is all a misunderstanding.*

"Even Jesus was persecuted, am I right, saints?"

Those words are all it takes for the congregation
to break out in a choir of
"Amens" and "Hallelujahs."

He continues the service,

"We will lean on Him to carry us through.
Tonight's Bible study will carry on."

Of course Pastor Johnson would ask the Bible study to continue. I guess even a devil knows damage control.

Everyone in this building worries they'll never see Pastor Johnson again. My worry is the arrest actually WAS a mistake and I WILL have to see him again.

Lately I've caught myself thinking about the day when Pastor Johnson would magically be taken out of my life. I even said a prayer about it a couple times. Maybe this is God doing the work for me. I don't have to speak about what happened that night, because maybe now, I won't have to worry about him at all.

I'm still left with all the feelings I don't understand. Like how now I'm worried about all the kids in my community who work for him to support their families. I look at him and see a villain but know there are elders who look at him and see the brightest aspect of their lives. Is it weird to actually feel bad for them? Why do I have to know him for everything that is evil, only for the world to only know him for everything good?

Maybe it's for tax fraud. The way he always carried cash, maybe he

SERVICE ENDS EARLY

I stop writing when I realize
for the first time in a long time,
a Holy Tabernacle services ends early.

A whole forty-five minutes early.

After thirty minutes of the assistant pastor's impromptu sermon,
he's already ending the night in prayer.

Slipping in a

> *Father God,*
> *we come to you humbly asking*
> *for you to carry our pastor through.*
> *For you to deliver him from evil,*
> *the way we know only you can.*
> *In your name we pray,*
> *Amen.*

DURING THE CAR RIDE HOME

my father calls the arrest a horrible mistake.

I say,

"Maybe there's a side of Pastor Johnson we don't kn—"

but he continues,

"Not possible. Pastor Johnson is a good man."

As if whatever he was arrested for couldn't possibly be true.

As if Pastor Johnson will only ever be remembered for all things good instead of the horrible things, that I know him for.

I keep my mouth shut   the way the world prefers.

MY MOTHER WAS A FIGHTER

My mother was a fighter—
it's in my blood.

I've never had a problem speaking up
and untying my tongue
to defend myself.

When a bank teller whispered under her breath
about my grandmother's broken English,
I spoke.

When my counselor threatened to take me out of Honors History
because of my behavior,
I fought.

But now,
when I need my voice to defend myself,
I can't.

All I know is a harrowing
silence.

My mother was a fighter;

I want nothing more than to believe:
It's in my blood.

MY MOTHER DIDN'T TELL ANYONE—

that she was going to the protest
and my family says, if they knew,
they would have tried to stop her

> but my mother was a fighter—
> she would have fought anyway

that night, her body
was engulfed by an accidental flame
in the land she loved

> a visit back home to see family,
> turned final goodbye

I was too young to remember
everything of her, but I remember
the way my heart shattered that night

> she promised
> it was only for a summer

she did not know
that was the only promise
she'd never keep.

FUEL TO THE FLAMES

My father raised me to believe
speaking up only adds
fuel to flames.

Tries to teach me the same
submission he has always known.
A submission my mother rebelled against.

When you are raised by a man
who believes silence is the safest garment
you learn to try on danger—
learn how to rip the restraints.

Either out of necessity
or rebellion.

But after that night,
I met a silence
I have never recognized.

How is this the only silence
I have ever worn?

TALIA CALLS

I glance at my phone to see six missed calls
and five unread texts from Talia.

A link to an article that reads:

"Maryland Pastor Randall Johnson Arrested on Sex Abuse Charges"

with messages that read:

Talia: Amina, I am so proud of you!

7:25 p.m.

Talia: Call me!

7:26 p.m.

Talia: When did you tell someone?

7:28 p.m.

Talia: Mina!!!

7:29 p.m.

Talia: CALL ME!!!!!!!!!!!!

7:33 p.m.

BREAKING: Maryland Pastor Randall Johnson Arrested on Sex Abuse Charges

Maryland pastor Randall Johnson has been arrested for the alleged sexual assault of a member from his church Holy Tabernacle.

Randall Johnson, 41, was appointed the position of senior pastor at Holy Tabernacle, the largest church in Baltimore City, following in his father's footsteps after his retirement. Police began investigating Johnson after the Baltimore City Police were recently alerted of the alleged assault. According to the 17-year-old victim, Randall Johnson sexually assaulted her beginning in May of last year.

Reporters contacted the church and the defense for comment but have yet to receive a response.

Authorities say the investigation is ongoing and anyone with information is asked to contact the Baltimore City Prosecutor's Office at 410-555-7297.

Comments:

AlliAlliOxenFree: I don't care who he is or what title he has. Right is right and wrong is wrong. This "pastor" is WRONG!

PrettyTrickyRicky: #FreeMyMansPastorJohnson! It's always when a man tries to do good for the COMMUNITY that y'all try to tear him down! Pastor Johnson gave me my first job when no one else would and I KNOW he's innocent! Y'all already know these bitches love to lie!

ChristeleK91: This man is supposed to be a pastor?! Shame on him AND Holy Tabernacle!

PositivelyPat: My heart goes out to this young lady. I experienced sexual assault as a teenager too. #YouareNOTalone

CharlesBeChillin: So . . . does this mean no more cookouts? I'm sorry but Pastor Johnson's cookouts really do be bomb! Those church folk can cook!

SisCarollSmith: I am a proud member of Holy Tabernacle and I know the Lord will carry my pastor through. No weapon formed against him shall prosper.

SonderSam: Shoutout to Pastor Johnson for getting arrested! I needed an excuse for my mom to let me miss church on Sundays!!!

SpeakTruth2Power: This girl is so brave and this man is embarrassing! My father is his age!

WHO?

Who could have po(**S**)sibly reported what happened?
The only person I've t(**o**)ld is Talia.

I read the article one (**m**)ore time,
only to r(**e**)alize the person in this article is seventeen—
and I don't turn seventeen until this summer.

This article says the assault to(**o**)k place last May—
but it didn't happe(**n**) until last month.

How could a n(**e**)ws article be so inaccurate?

I must hav(**E**) read the artic(**l**)e three times
before it finally dawn(**s**) on m(**e**).

I text Talia:

Amina: There is someone else.

Katie Walbrook: All right, so I understand that you learned about Randall Johnson's arrest during a weekly Bible study. I want to speak about your teacher Ms. Hamilton. You chose to confide in her, correct?

Amina Conteh: Does it really matter if I'm here?

Katie Walbrook: I just want to make sure we are covering all bases. Is she the only teacher you spoke to about this matter?

Amina Conteh: Yes, and if I never did I wouldn't have to be here right now.

Katie Walbrook: I understand this is difficult, but you're doing the right thing today.

Amina Conteh: Mhm—or yes, I guess.

Katie Walbrook: Okay, so you told Ms. Harold—

Amina Conteh: You mean Ms. Hamilton.

Katie Walbrook: Thank you for correcting me, Amina. I understand you confided in your teacher, Ms. Hamilton. What happened after you confided in her?

JANUARY 22:
5 WEEKS AFTER THE ASSAULT

SNEAKY LINK

Ever since my father found out about my grades,
        Deon and I have been more careful while sneaking around.

Today we're meeting at a park
        fifteen minutes away from my place.

Close enough for me to leave if my father calls,
        far enough for him to not see me with Deon.

"Honestly, Mina, I ain't too mad at having to sneak around.
        It makes the time I do spend with you more important."

I like these moments with Deon,
        when we don't have to say much to enjoy each other's space.

It gives me a happy place to rest in,
        where I don't have to think about what my life has become.

But maybe Deon doesn't enjoy silence as much as I do—

DEON ASKS A QUESTION

"Mina, cool if I talk to you about something that's been on my mind?"

Questions begin to swirl around in my head:

Are my hands too sweaty to hold?

> *Have I been too distant?*

>> *Does he want to break up?*

He continues,

"I still can't get my head around my uncle's arrest.
Everyone in the city knew him for doing good, you know?"

I shrug   force a smile.
Most times, if you let people do the talking,
they don't realize you're not speaking at all.

He continues,

"My mom doesn't believe it.
Says that she knows her brother would never do that.
But I'm not sure that somebody would just lie like that,
you know what I mean?"

I force another smile. This time,
my mouth feels harder to move.

"Yeah, I know what you mean."

Deon asks how I've been holding up since the news.
I shrug
not because I don't have anything to say,
but because *I don't know what to say.*

I do not say,

*Your mother choosing to believe your uncle
means she would probably choose not to believe me.*

I do not say,

I am unsure if you would believe me either.

I do not say,

This is another reason on the list of reasons why I won't speak.

When I find words,
I say,

"You look great. I'm glad we get to hang today."

He squeezes my hand   and kisses me,
and it's great.

His lips are soft,
he's gentle the way he always is—
so I don't understand why it's so hard to kiss him back.

Deon's right.

People *do* know Pastor Johnson for doing good for the city.
& barely anybody in this city knows me at all.

How is it that I could go the longest I've ever gone
without seeing Pastor Johnson since we joined that damn church
and *still* be reminded of him more than I ever have?

I WANT TO

"Did I do something wrong, Mina?
It kind of seems like you didn't really want to kiss me."

I want to talk to Deon.

I want to tell him,

You didn't do anything. Your uncle did,

but my mouth never allows.

Instead, I grab my things.
Say,

"I just realized I have classwork to make up.
Wouldn't want to get in trouble again.
See you tomorrow."

THE NEXT DAY AT SCHOOL

My options for lunch are limited.
I can either:

> **A.** eat alone in the cafeteria and give people
> another reason to talk shit.

> or

> **B.** eat lunch with Ms. Hamilton in the comfort
> of a student-less room.

Talia is absent with a cold
& Deon is retaking a biology exam.

Holy Holly asked to eat together
but I don't want to spend my lunch with her either.

Ms. Hamilton has offered to have lunch with me to "talk"
four times since the last time Bowl Cut ran his mouth.

So, I choose:

> **B.** eat lunch with Ms. Hamilton in the comfort
> of a student-less room.

MS. HAMILTON'S ROOM FOR LUNCH IT IS

Before I knock on Ms. Hamilton's door,
I get a text message.

Holly: Hey, I know you said you're busy during lunch today

but maybe we can hang after school?

I ignore the message.

The last thing I want is a hangout-with-Holy-Holly
turned Holy-Tabernacle-Youth-Choir-recruitment meeting
while she tells me that Sister Patty

just really needs more voices.

Doesn't matter I tell her I'm never going,
she always feels the need to

just ask.

Before I respond,
Ms. Hamilton sees me at the door and invites me in.

MS. HAMILTON OPENS THE DOOR

and asks me how I'm doing.

I cannot manage to take my mouth off mute.

She doesn't try to shoo me away.
She brings out her lunch for the day—a salad.

Probably Caesar

During debate practice, she used to stuff her face with them,
always managing to soil some article of clothing.

"IT   NEEDS   MORE   DRESSING!"

she would shout with her mouth half open.

She opens a desk full of granola bars, fruit snacks, and waters,
points at them, signaling me to have my pick.

I grab a water and peanut butter Chewy bar,
still not speaking.

Ms. Hamilton looks up from her salad and says:

"I'm happy you could join me for lunch today."

I nod, still silent,
scarfing a Chewy bar down my throat.

"I spoke with your father about your grades slipping.
He said you've been pretty affected by the arrest of Randall Johnson—"

Hearing his name makes my body   jolt,

while my mind forgets where I am.

MIND YOUR DAMN BUSINESS

I told Ms. Hamilton: she should mind her damn business

She tells me: she and my father are only concerned

I tell her: her concern doesn't do shit for me

She tells me: she understands the arrest must be hard

I tell her: she has no idea what she's talking about

She says: *I understand you looked up to him*

She thinks *I look up to* that man.

EVERYONE AROUND ME

thinks that man

                    is
                    someone
                    to
                    look
                    up
                    to

thinks his good deeds can

                wash   away   any   and   every   sin

I mumble under my breath,

Pastor Johnson ain't shit.
You in love with him or some shit?

I try to grab my things and leave

                        but my books—and my body—

                feel too weak to carry
                and the heaviest tears
                stream
                down
                my
                face.

I DIDN'T PLAN ON IT

Maybe Deon and Holly always wanting to talk about him
causes me to want to open my mouth.

Maybe the thought that anyone would believe I could ever miss him
makes me want to tell the whole world why nobody should.

Maybe knowing how wonderful this city—including my father—
thinks that man is (& how awful I know he is) forces me to speak.

In a single breath I tell Ms. Hamilton what happened
before I regret I tell her all I remember

ALL I REMEMBER (CENSORED)

MS. HAMILTON TELLS ME

Ms. Hamilton tells me I am not alone.

Where she's from everyone got a story,
and anybody who doesn't,
knows three girls who do.

       Ms. Hamilton tells me I am brave.

       I should be proud of speaking up and sharing my truth
       I should be proud of the last five minutes of my life
       many people in my position never experience them.

Ms. Hamilton says all this only to eventually say:

"I'll contact your teachers to excuse you for the day.
We'll be heading to guidance to begin filing a report."

MANDATED REPORTER

is what Ms. Hamilton says she is

> *Mandated reporter*
> is a term the school uses to say
> teachers & faculty members are
> required to report
> anything that may cause a child to
> "be in danger"

Mandated reporter
is a term for teachers to use,
to wipe their hands of anything
that could get themselves in trouble

> *Mandated reporter*
> is what Ms. Hamilton says when I say
> she's forcing me to tell my business

I tell her:

it doesn't make a difference.
He's in jail and wouldn't be able to hurt me
or anyone else anyway
but Ms. Hamilton

> kept saying those same damned words

Mandated reporter = Snitch

> *Mandated reporter* = Ms. Hamilton

I TOLD HER I WOULD LIE

I would say *it didn't happen.*
I made everything up.

Ms. Hamilton only says:
"None of this is your fault.
I have to report this information."

I tell her that's bullshit

Ms. Hamilton says she is "so sorry"
this happened to me but either I
must report
or *she'll do it herself.*

It doesn't matter how much I beg

Ms. Hamilton says her obligation is
to report
and contact my father.

I TRIED TO LIE

While walking to the guidance office,
I send a text to Talia:

Amina: I told someone. Hope you're happy.

When Ms. Hamilton & I walk inside,
there is a worn-out gray sofa in the corner of the room
Ms. Hamilton tells me to have a seat
while she walks over to the guidance counselor.

Their tones, hushed, but their body language—
worried eyes and furrowed brows—speaks loudly.

They walk over to me.
The guidance counselor's voice is soft when she says,
"Ms. Hamilton told me a bit of what brings you here today."

> My voice breaks when I whisper
> *Ms. Hamilton has no idea*
> *what she's talking about.*

The guidance counselor asks,
"What happened that night?"

> I say *nothing happened that night.*

The guidance counselor asks,
"What would make you feel
comfortable right now?"

> I tell her *nothing would make me*
> *comfortable right now.*

The guidance counselor asks
if I'd like to wait for my father.

> I cry
>
> Say *nothing at all.*

I TELL THE TRUTH

The guidance counselor must have contacted my father
somewhere between me crying and me saying nothing.

Within twenty minutes he walks into the room.
The nail-biting habit I kicked three years ago resurfaces.
& my leg will not
                          stop
                          shaking.

Ms. Hamilton lays a hand on my shoulder
and tells me I am safe
but I'm still crushed
                          by
                          the weight
                          of setting my own secret   free.

I close my eyes to avoid the way
my father's face twists while he hears
about what the man he's admired for years did.
My mouth becomes a reluctant fountain,
                                          as
                                          my
                                          story
                                          spills.

Between sobs I blurt
                          everything
                          I remember

until I start to feel myself want to vomit.

AS I FINISH, I OPEN MY EYES

I silently congratulate myself
on the last ten minutes
of my life.

Like Ms. Hamilton said,
A lot of survivors will never experience them.

I spoke up.

The guidance counselor sits, eyes wide,
as if she can't find the words she's trained to have.

Ms. Hamilton tries
and fails
to hold back tears.

My father is looking at the floor,
searching for the words anyone
who goes through anything,
knows will never be enough.

Finally, my father tells me how much he cares about me—

but I will never forget the next words he said.

THE NEXT WORDS HE SPOKE TO ME:

I just don't get it.

Pastor Johnson is a good man.

Are you sure there wasn't a misunderstanding?

MY COURAGE DISAPPEARS

When my father says these words,
it's as if any courage I conjured today   disappears.

Like my voice doesn't matter.

I watch all my words   flee   like my best magic trick.

Glance at my phone,
realize I never checked Talia's response—

Talia: I'm just seeing this. I've been in bed sick all day.

Love you Mina. Everything will work out.

Proud of you, here for you, and love you for life.

WE DO NOT SPEAK

That night my father asks me to do the dishes
by pointing to the used ones in the sink—
                                   without speaking.

Tells me he is proud of the A essay I leave on the counter
with a head nod and half a smile—
                                   without speaking.

Tells me rice and stew are ready on the stove
by making his own plate for dinner—
                                   without speaking.

How can he listen when all he's ever known is a never-ending silence?

I do not know why I expected to be heard
by a man who knows silence
better than he knows
his pastor
or a loved one.

                        Even his daughter.

A SURVIVOR, HIS DAUGHTER, OR A DEVIL?

My father worshipped Johnson like a god.

Wonder if I kept my mouth shut
if my father would still find salvation in Him.

Wonder if my father still remembers Johnson

> Whenever he *thinks* of God
> Whenever he *prays* to God
> Whenever he *cries* to God

I think of my father

> Whenever I am *angry* with God
> Whenever I am *hurt* by God
> Whenever I *hate* God

Does that make me:

> a survivor?
> his daughter?
> or
> a devil?

101 DALMATIANS

When I get home, I work on a puzzle my mom used to love.

101 Dalmatians.

After twenty minutes, I wash my face, brush my teeth,
and slip on a nightgown she used to wear.

I head to bed
and play her favorite hymn

"His Eye Is on the Sparrow"

LOSING HIS RELIGION

When you lose a parent at a young age
all you have are the stories people tell
and blurred memories.

I've heard stories of her persistence from relatives.
My uncle says when they were young,

> she would fight anyone who ever tried to hurt him;
> she would defend everyone around her before herself.

The day my mother died is the day my father lost his religion.

After she passed, my father and I woke

> later and later

and attended services

> later and later

until we eventually didn't see the inside of a church for months.

MY MOTHER'S HAVEN

My mother used to drag both my father and me to church.
Always said:

"No family of mine will have their ass in bed
on Sunday mornings when we have a God to praise!"

Church was her:

Safe Haven
Book Club
Gossip Group
and Therapy

But ever since she told a church minister
he could "go to hell!"
in front of a parking lot of saints
because he "joked"
the dress she put me in was
"a little too short for service,"

I'm not sure if she loved church
as much as she was comfortable with the idea of it.

Because that's how her mother was
and her mother's mother.

I never really felt a part of the church,
always felt like my thoughts were too wild,
my tongue too slick.

But the church was a part of her,
like a second home.

Which made a part of me *want* to move in too.

I AIN'T EVER TELL ANYONE

but I always wondered if it was my mother's love
for church—or just her low tolerance for bullshit—
that actually held our family together.

Ever since Pastor Johnson invited us back
to church for a "family night"
of dinner and games, which eventually turned
into a recruitment night
with him telling us how he and *The Good Lord*
want us back in his home,

it's like my father has found God again
like he found a love he's only known in my mom,

one that I've never given.

EVERY SUNDAY MORNING SINCE PASTOR JOHNSON

convinced my father that God—and my mother—
would want us back in the holy house,
my father wakes, and the same words blow
through our apartment like a faithful wind:

Mina, you can't get out of bed one day a week for Jesus?!

Often I see my father
raising his hand in worship
or kneeling in prayer,

Mina, if you don't hurry, we're going to be late!

But sometimes I wonder if my father
ever forgets who God is,
like I do when I am angry.
I wonder if he ever doubts—

MINA!

until it's the week of my mother's death.

When he's reading the Bible
and chanting prayers every chance he gets—
as if it could miraculously bring her back.

Ain't it funny how death can make people find faith
in a God they barely believed in?

THE DAY HE LOST MY MOTHER

                is the day he lost his religion

The day he found Pastor Johnson

                is the day he found his religion

& the day I lost myself

                I've been searching

          ever
                s
                i
                n
                c
                e

THE FIRST FULL SENTENCE

My father heads to bed, without **(S)**peaking
about what happened in the guidance office.

Later that night I g**(o)** to the kitchen
for a glass of water & find my father
at the dining room table,
c**(r)**ying,
with the same Bible in hand.

He looks up,
says the first full sentence since leaving the school,
offe**(r)**ing words I have never heard
in this home—

M**(y)** father says:

"I'm sorry."

"SORRY."

Words

                  are

    never

enough

                  to

        clean

                        a

    mess

after

                  it's

        made.

JANUARY 24
10:52 A.M.

Katie Walbrook: Are you prepared to continue the interview, or would you like another break?

Amina Conteh: I'm prepared.

Katie Walbrook: Okay. Can you describe the night of the assault?

DECEMBER 19:
THE ASSAULT

MY MOUTH WILL NOT ALLOW ME TO MAKE A SOUND

I try to focus on anything else.
The worn-out carpet.
The stain on the desk chair.

My eyes lock on a painting of the Virgin Mary.

NEVER ASKED

Just a couple of Sundays ago, Johnson said:

The world knows Mary for being the mother of Jesus.
A woman chosen by God to give a miraculous virgin birth.

I know Mary faced a world full of judgment,
being tasked with bearing a burden she never asked for,
but the pastor never tells the story that way.

On this day, I know Mary
as a woman whose story will forever serve as my mirror. During
every communion   every family dinner   every holiday season

I'll never be tasked to birth a savior,
but both Mary and I did endure   a reckoning.

IN THE BIBLE

Mary had a man named Joseph,
who didn't believe her when she told him
she wasn't carrying another man's son but
the Son of Man.

The story continues,
God told Joseph himself.
Confirmed for him,
Mary wasn't lying through a dream—

as if a woman's word is never enough.

MOTHER MARY

Right now, I feel like Mary.

But Pastor Johnson *is not the God*
his congregation makes him out to be.

When I was younger, I didn't understand
how God could give Mary a kid.

Would that make God the father?

and if he was,

How could God give Mary Jesus
without her consent?

HOLY TREND AMONG HOLY MEN

Is this a trend among the holy men?
Giving "gifts" us women didn't ask for?

A HORRIBLE, HORRIBLE MISTAKE

During the ride home
I pretend this is a mistake,
convince myself
what I experienced couldn't be real.

*This is all some sort of dream,
Pastor Johnson couldn't possibly be capable
of doing what he did to me.*

> *Maybe I was at the wrong place,
> at the wrong time,
> in the wrong body.*

> *Maybe if I close my eyes,
> and dream hard enough,
> I can transport myself*

> *far   far   far*

> *from here.*

MARY, DID YOU KNOW?

The ride home is silent
besides radio-station Christmas music.

A version of the carol "Mary, Did You Know?"
recorded before I was born plays.

The son of a bitch couldn't even play
the version by Mary J. Blige.

THIRD SNOWFALL

Today is the third snowfall of the season,
but my body is so hot,
my palms and forehead
are sweating.

Out the window, a darkness
only lit by the occasional decorated home
or functioning streetlight
covers the city.

More lights aren't working tonight than usual.

The ones that do work blend together
when the car moves quickly.   A blur
still clearer than how I feel.

The only sound I can make
is the gritting of my own teeth.
Pastor Johnson doesn't speak
but wears a smirk on his face
as if we experienced two different nights.

THREE HUNDRED DOLLARS

I only realize I am home because the car stops moving.

Johnson hands me three hundred dollars,
one hundred and fifty dollars more than promised.
Must be his way of saying,

Thank you.

ALONE

My father is not
in the living room
but his Bible
is still on the counter.

I head to my room,
close the door
behind me.

Grab my journal
for the first time
outside of church service.

December 19

Nobody knows what they would do when something like this happens. But I always imagined I'd fight back, and claw my fingers right through his face until I broke the skin.

But I laid there. As if my body was glued to the floor. Like my mind begged to take itself anywhere other than where I was, and I wanted to protect the girl who's still there but just . . . couldn't.

It was as if I was stuck in the world's worst movie.

And I am still waiting for the show to finally end.

DEON TEXTS ME

Deon: Hey Mina! I'm guessing you forgot to call

and you're asleep right now?

Just checking in on you. I'll see you tomorrow!

I turn off my phone

I go to sleep

pretend I am   anywhere

feeling anything

other than what I do now.

<u>Katie Walbrook:</u> I think I have everything I need for right now. Thank you, Amina.

<u>Amina Conteh:</u> Thanks, I guess.

<u>Katie Walbrook:</u> This will conclude our formal interview.

FEBRUARY 11:

2½ WEEKS AFTER THE POLICE INTERVIEW

UPWARDS OF A YEAR

Detective Walbrook says trials usually take
upwards of a year in our district.

That I'm "lucky" to have a trial
scheduled seven months after a police interview.

Detective Walbrook says because the case involves minors
and Johnson is a popular community figure,
this case is a priority in our district.

The trial date is August 12.

There are exactly 182 days left until the trial.

I'M ALL OUT OF EXCUSES.

Every other time Talia begged me to come to The Shack
I've told her I have too much schoolwork
or was too tired to leave the house.

But after school today, the guilt trip was so heavy,
and I fumbled my thoughts so bad,
the only word left in my vocabulary was an unenthusiastic

"Okay."

While Talia rambles about a sale at the mall,
I can't help but notice The Shack is less familiar today.
I can't help but notice Holly isn't working here anymore.

Holly was absent half of last month,
and the rumor is after Holy Tabernacle went under fire
her family found a new church.

TALIA FINALLY CAME CLEAN

"So, how about the mall this weekend?
Maybe I can even invite Julia and you can meet each other!"

Talia finally fessed up her feelings toward Julia
and now she is her crush-turned-girlfriend.
I'd rather pass on being the third wheel.

Talia continues:

"You know, get your mind off of things—
I mean. Only if you want to. It's okay if you don't."

Talia doesn't joke with me anymore.
She used to crack the most inappropriate jokes,
always at the most appropriate times.

Now she's overly cautious,
always trying to fix a broken person like me.

"I'll pass."

Talia nods, disappointed.

I know she feels she doesn't know her friend anymore.
But lately, I don't know myself anymore.

She looks up toward the door before saying:

"Well, are you up for seeing Deon?"

DEON AND I HAVEN'T SPOKEN ABOUT IT

But after the news reported a second girl being assaulted,
he kept asking me if I was okay as if he knew.

I lied.

I told him I didn't know the second girl.
That I couldn't believe this could happen to someone else,
not telling him the "someone" was me.

"I don't know if I want to see him, Talia."

Talia points to the door,

"Well, you better make up your mind now,
because he just walked in."

DEON WALKS OVER TO US

and says,

"Hey, Mina. Hey, Talia.
How are you today?"

Talia tells him we're okay
and asks him about some history assignment they have.
I keep my eyes glued to the table,
wishing I never left my room.

"Well, I guess I'll see you both in school tomorrow.
Mina, cool if I text you later?
You've been on my mind a lot lately."

I nod, eyes still on the table,
only looking up as he walks away.

HE WOULDN'T UNDERSTAND

"Mina, I know it's hard, but Deon would understand.
Plus.
He told me he misses you."

I want to believe Talia is right.
Truth is,
I don't know if Deon would understand.
A part of me thinks he'd respond just like his mother did.

"Hey, Talia, is it all right if we hang tomorrow instead?
I'm not feeling too well. Might be something I ate."

Talia's eyes widen and she tightens her lips,
the way she always does when she doesn't know
how to say what she wants to.

"Julia and I actually have a date tomorrow."

She says the latter half of the sentence slowly
before staring at the floor.
She adds,

"But you're totally welcome to—"

I tell her it's fine.
That I have to go. Grab my coat,
my bag,
walk out the door before she finishes.

Every time we hang, it feels like the beginning
of the end of the friendship I had with her.
& the beginning of a lifetime of her spending
every waking moment
                    hanging with
                    talking about
                    & obsessing over
                    Julia

I can't call Deon because he thinks
I don't want to talk to him anymore—which is still less difficult
than telling the truth about *why I'*m not talking to him anymore.

Truth is,
I don't know how to talk,
to anyone
anymore.

& I'm starting to wonder if I even want to.

POLICE INTERVIEW TRANSCRIPT:
TALIA ARIAS
FEBRUARY 12
11:09 A.M.

Katie Walbrook: Hi, Talia, right? How are you?

Talia Arias: Yes, that's my name. I'm doing all right.

Katie Walbrook: Well first, I want to say thank you to you and your mother for bringing you here to speak with me. A lot of parents choose to have their children not get involved in these kinds of cases, but Talia's report today is going to be super helpful in building Amina's case.

Elisa Arias: Of course. Talia and Amina have been friends for so long, it breaks my heart to know she's going through this, and if Talia can help, I'm happy to comply.

Talia Arias: Yeah, it's still hard to think about sometimes honestly.

Katie Walbrook: Well, we're going to do our best to make sure we build the strongest case possible. Talia, according to Amina, you are the first person she confided in. Is this true?

Talia Arias: Yes, she confided in me a few days before reporting to you.

Katie Walbrook: So I understand that Amina spoke with you first, but she went just over a month after the incident without speaking to anyone. During that time, do you have any idea why Amina chose not to speak?

Talia Arias: Well—I don't—I knew something was wrong but every time I asked she said she was okay. I don't know—maybe it's because it would have been hard for her?

Elisa Arias: I don't think it's very fair for my daughter to have to answer that question. Amina is a sixteen-year-old girl and I'm sure between us, Detective Walbrook, we can both agree there are plenty of things that we did not speak with our parents about. And especially not with the police about. Correct?

Katie Walbrook: My apologies. I just want to make sure we are as thorough as possible so we are prepared for any counterarguments from the defense. Talia, can you tell me if there were any changes in Amina's behavior before she confided in you?

Talia Arias: Well, yeah actually. She became pretty quiet and kept to herself. But I always thought it had something to do with her dad. You know, the fact that they don't get along sometimes.

Katie Walbrook: Amina and her father don't get along? Can you explain that a bit?

Talia Arias: Yeah, well Amina and her dad don't talk to each other much. And she doesn't talk about him much either. She's always made it seem like they don't have the best relationship.

Katie Walbrook: Can you elaborate on them not getting along?

Talia Arias: That's all I really know. I guess—maybe because he's really quiet—she doesn't talk much about him. I-I'm sorry. I guess I don't know as much about her as I thought.

Katie Walbrook: You've provided more than enough. Is there anything else that you think might be helpful for us to know?

Talia Arias: Not that I can think of right now. I just want my friend to be okay.

SAME SOFA, SAME TEA, SAME DAMN BOOK

I come home and my father is on that same sofa,
drinking that same cup of tea,
reading that same. damn. book.

I used to feel bad for him.
When you lose a love—
the only woman you've ever loved—
sometimes you lose yourself,
and that's what happened with my father.

He never learned to love again.

My dad may have liked church,
but my mom *loved it*.
After her death, it's as if loving God
was the last way he knew how to love my mother.

He wrapped himself in the teachings of a god
who I'm unsure he originally believed in.

WHAT MY MOTHER BELIEVED IN

My mother believed in God with her whole heart,
but she also believed in
love,
laughter,
dance.

My father used to dance with her.
Sometimes I would just watch,
but other times I would dance with them too.

Sometimes my mother retired her gospel music,
and traded it for soul, R&B, jazz,
or her favorite, Stevie Wonder.
Letting *Songs in the Key of Life*
fill our home and our hearts.

But when my mother passed,
my dad lost
his spark,
his rhythm,
his way.

MY FATHER DOESN'T DANCE

He no longer dances.

Just sits on that *same sofa,*
drinking that *same cup of tea,*
reading that
Same.
Damn.
Book.

When he notices I'm home,
he asks about my day and his eyes never leave his Bible.

I almost answer,
until his phone rings with a call from work,
and I sneak to my room knowing he'll forget he ever asked.

A reminder of how easy it is to be invisible in a home
where the only person you live with ain't checkin' for you no way.

SAME OLD STORY

The news articles have been the hardest.

I know it doesn't serve me to read the same recycled articles,
but even on nights when I promise myself I won't look,
I end up scrolling on my phone.
Worrying about everything I know I'll never be able to control.

Tonight is no different.

When I first pressed charges, a new article released every day.
The press has slowed down, but occasionally
a news outlet comes late to the party and reports the same old news.

Some outlets describe me and the other survivor as teenage girls,
some reveal our ages.
But every article has had a vague description.
Every article until the one I find tonight:

BREAKING: Trial Date Has Been Set After Second Victim Comes Forward with Sex Abuse Claims Against Maryland Pastor Randall Johnson

A trial date in the ongoing case against popular community figure and pastor Randall Johnson has been set for August 12 after a second victim came forward.

Police began investigating Johnson after the first victim, a 17-year-old girl identified as **HR**, contacted Baltimore City Police on January 17.

The second victim, identified as **AC**, came forward on January 24 claiming that Randall Johnson sexually assaulted her in December of last year.

Bail is currently set at $200,000.

Our reporters contacted Holy Tabernacle and the defense for comment but have yet to receive a response.

Anyone with any additional information is asked to contact Baltimore City Prosecutor's office at 410-555-7297.

Comments:

MarissaHill17: I knew something was off with him. My mom and I left Holy Tabernacle and that nasty pastor weeks ago. We support the survivors!

PapaBear87: I'll tell you what, I wouldn't let these girls around my children. I've read up on this man and he's done great things. Now all of a sudden, this news is coming out? I'll believe it once I see a verdict.

BritBaker: Wait, I know two people who used to go to that church with those initials. No way this pastor did this to them!

AskAaron: No disrespect but you all do know he isn't guilty right? And doesn't this article say the first incident happened months ago? Why wait until now? We have to hear both sides.

BookABoo: Why would a survivor lie about this? Maybe you should try believing survivors before you assume they're lying. I stand WITH these girls. Not against them.

MandyMaddy: LOL, too bad he can't wear suits in jail where he belongs. LOCK HIM UP!!!!

Natty3000: Two sides to every story. Imma wait for the facts.

JTLovesPJ: Two sides to every story? What other side could there possibly be when the girls are minors? How about believing women when they speak up?

REACHING OUT

I only know one seventeen-year-old girl at Holy Tabernacle
with the initials "HR"
Holly Robertson.

This explains why she wasn't at Bible study that night
and why up until my father and I stopped going to Holy Tabernacle,
I didn't see much of her or her family during services.

Amina: Hey Holly, I saw an article in the paper about my case

My initials were released.

It also released the initials "HR"

Give me a call?

If you told me two months ago,
I would be reaching out to Holly,
I wouldn't believe you.

Lately the only person in the world
who could possibly understand what I'm going through
is the only person who's going through all this with me.
And now I know that person is

Holly.

But ten minutes pass by,
and she doesn't respond.
Then an hour passes,
then two,
then three.

Maybe Holly doesn't feel the same.

Holly Robertson: I told you I don't have anything to say.

Katie Walbrook: Holly. It's okay to be fearful. What you're doing is incredibly brave.

Holly Robertson: I don't want to be brave. I want to go home.

Katie Walbrook: I'll try to make this as quick as possible. I just wanted to follow up on a couple of claims you made in your report in January.

Holly Robertson: What report?

Katie Walbrook: I understand you're hurt. I'm not trying to make this difficult for you, Holly.

Holly Robertson: I want to go home.

Katie Walbrook: You came to us with your family to report an assault by Randall Johnson on the morning of January seventeenth. Are you now saying that never happened?

Holly Robertson: I'm saying I want to go home.

HUSH MONEY

After Johnson's arrest,
Holy Tabernacle offered us settlement money
to have their name completely disassociated with the case.

Otherwise known as

Hush Money.

In order to receive the settlement,
I signed an agreement saying Johnson's actions
are separate from the church
and that any criminal charges will proceed with just him.

They washed away responsibility,
like a sinner washes away their sins.

DOLLARS. ONE HUNDRED THOUSAND OF THEM.

When I get home from school today,
my father isn't home.
But a note on the counter reads:

Your money came today.

$100,000.

Most will be saved for your college fund.

Until then, I will give you an allowance.

—Dad

The note has a one-hundred-dollar bill attached,
and I already know how to spend it.

BONE STRAIGHT

If I know one thing about Talia,
I know she's always down for a makeover.

After I got the money, I called her.

Our friendship has been rocky since our last time at The Shack,
but neither of us has brought it up.
Just glossed past   kept pushing.
It's been easier that way.

I asked her if her aunt would be willing to see me at her salon today.
Within ten minutes she pulled up outside to give me a ride,
already on the phone asking her aunt to hook me up
and before I knew it, I was sitting in a salon chair.

"I want something completely different.
I want it bone straight.
With highlights.
Yellow highlights."

THE BIG CHOP

I haven't gotten my hair done at a salon since I was six,
after I took a pair of scissors to my hair
because I saw a photo of Janet Jackson & wanted hair just like hers.

Only issue is Ms. Janet was rocking a non-parental-approved mullet.

I don't remember much of the scissors.
Or the chopping.
Or even the mullet.

But I do remember being driven to a salon,
having most of my hair chopped off.

The whole room watching as my afro,
once bigger than my head,
made its way to the floor, inch by inch.

I remember crying.
Thinking *nobody wants to play*
with the ugly girl on the playground.

I don't remember much of my mother outside of the stories.
But I remember she told me I was beautiful that day.
That I wear the most gorgeous cheekbones she's ever seen.
I remember her cutting her hair the next week,
so I would believe it to be true.

I remember thinking maybe she was right.

BUT I CAN *FEEL* BEAUTIFUL ANY DAY

Today I want to be different.
A day for something new.
Something other than that night in December.

As Talia's aunt does my hair,
the smell of grease and smoke fill the room.

"One more pass with the flat iron,
and we'll be done."

When Talia's aunt finishes my hair,
she turns me around in the salon chair to face the mirror.

My hair,
once standing tall on top of my head,
now falling down my back.
Flowing whenever a breeze tells it to.
With yellow tints peeking through.

Talia's aunt says the words I've been waiting to hear:

"You look *good,* ma."

I KNEW I LOOKED GOOD TOO.

So did Talia and the rest of the people in the salon,
watching me whip my hair
like a rich boy whips a brand-new convertible.

Talia says,

"I hope you feel as good as you look."

Why feel good when you can convince
everyone in the world you *look good* instead?

EVERYONE EXCEPT MY FATHER

I secretly hoped he would like it.
At the very least, I thought he would have an opinion.
That he would hate it or think it was stupid.
That he would tell me to march back to the salon and change it back.

But he stares at me.
Like his daughter gained three heads instead of a dye job.

"Is this how you're choosing to spend your money?
It seems like a waste. But if you think it's nice."

& he continues with his day,
like the ghost of a father he's always been.

I continue about mine,
as the invisible daughter I'll always be.

Amina: Hey Holly, how's everything going?

This has been really hard on both of us.

I guess I'm reaching out to say I know what you're going through,

and I hope you're holding up okay.

HOUSE SOUNDTRACK

The local news was our 5:00 p.m. soundtrack,
but after my news broke my father ignored the TV for days.
Now, the only time those channels come on
is when the *Simpsons* reruns play.

I know every episode better than my class material these days.

The show writers are so good they need a raise too.
The show was written before I was born
but predicted the invention of video calls,
Super Bowl winners, and even smartwatches.
In one episode, they even predicted
conspiracy theories about rigged voting systems.

I've learned to predict the future too:
It's 6:00 p.m. and my father hasn't mentioned dinner yet.
I know this means we're having pizza tonight. This time,
he sits at the table instead of taking his plate to his room.

It's not every night we have dinner together,
but he's been trying more than he used to.
My father speaks about the latest dental office drama:

"People get angry like you're the one billing them.
I'm just the man who tells you!"

I nod,
and as I start to tell him about my classes, his phone rings—
one of the oldest members of Holy Tabernacle is calling.

We haven't spoken to anyone from Holy Tabernacle in months
but she was one of the only members
of Holy Tabernacle to publicly defend me.
I call her Seasoned Saint.

My father's phone is set so loud I can hear every word:

PHONE CALL WITH SEASONED SAINT

Seasoned Saint: Nigel, have you seen the news?

> **Dad:** No, I haven't in a while now.

Seasoned Saint: Johnson.

He made bail! You and Mina aren't still—

> **Dad:** He what?!

Seasoned Saint: Turn on the news and watch for yourself!

Is she doing okay?

We've all been thinking about her—

> **Dad:** I've got to go.

MY FATHER YELLS

As soon as my father hangs up the phone
he asks if I overheard his conversation.

I nod, he heads to his room
and calls the district's prosecutor's office, yelling.

"Why would you not tell us about this?
This upsets my daughter and me!"

My father walks back into the dining room,
mumbling under his breath in that way
that makes his face scrunch real tight,
like he's tasted two-month-old sour milk.

He holds his hand over the speaker—
as if that has ever stopped anyone
from hearing anything, ever.

"I can't believe they wouldn't tell us!
I told them it upset you and they have nothing
to say for themselves! They should be ashamed!"

My father takes the call back to his room.
His voice trailing as he closes the door behind him.

JOHNSON MAKING BAIL SURPRISES MY FATHER—

but not me.
The way he used to fling money around,
I'm surprised he didn't make bail earlier.

What surprises me is my fear.

What if I run into him on the street?
What if he finds me and tries to hurt me?
What if my father is angry enough to hurt him?

One moment I'm proud
of doing the thing you're supposed to do.
For standing up and telling my truth,
and all the other empowering shit I've read online.

But during these moments, I am an exposed wound
for everyone to gawk at. The kind that never heals
and leaves the deepest scar you can never explain.

My father finally ends his phone call and leaves his room.
Says,

"You're not going to school tomorrow.
If that man can walk around freely,
they'll have to explain themselves to us."

THE SECOND MISSED DAY SINCE SEVENTH GRADE

The first day I reported what happened
was the first day of school my father's allowed me to miss
since my seventh-grade food poisoning.

Just like that.
I'll be able to say I've missed *two* days of school
since the seventh grade.

Deon: Hey Mina, I watched something on the news

and I'm really worried about you.

I care about you and want you to be okay.

Call me when you get this?

MARCH 23: 142 DAYS UNTIL TRIAL

A SLOW DAY AT THE STATION

"You all are fools to grant that man bail to begin with!
How is Amina supposed to feel safe with him around?"

I know I'm not the only kid whose parent
has kept them from going to school.

It's just usually those kids are kept home
because they're sick, or for a doctor's appointment—
not to watch their father yell at an entire prosecutor's office.

Today must be a slow day.
So far, I've seen only two people come into the station.

One person only speaks between hysterical cries,
the other reports a stolen engagement ring.
Six carats, according to her.

My father's fists are balled as if he is ready to fight.
He grits his teeth in a way I've never seen.

I wait in a seat in the lobby
while my father and Detective Walbrook
step away for a "private conversation."

A private conversation about my now-public business.

I'M USED TO BEING THE ONE WHO ALWAYS WANTS

to kick,
to scream,
to fight.

But after that night,
I don't know how anymore.

Like he stole all my happiness
and my fearlessness too.

Detective Walbrook asks us to follow her to a private room.
Says everyone at the station couldn't believe Johnson made bail.
Before she finally says:

"There is one development in the case
I do need to speak to you about before you leave."

Katie Walbrook: Thank you, Holly, for agreeing to speak with me one more time. And thank you, Mrs. Robertson, for agreeing to bring her in today.

Nicole Robertson: Not a problem.

Katie Walbrook: Now, Holly, I understand that these cases are stressful. But I have to ask, are you sure that—

Holly Robertson: I don't know how many times I have to tell you I'm sure before you get it.

Katie Walbrook: I understand. It's just, we're building a pretty strong case and—

Holly Robertson: I said I want out. I don't want to do this anymore. All the questions, rumors, comments. About me? About my family? This doesn't feel like justice to me and I want out.

Katie Walbrook: I understand. It's just—

Nicole Robertson: Detective, with all due respect, I think it's best that Holly and I go home. Holly is just starting to find her balance again. She's at a new school, we're in a new church, and a new neighborhood. And with the settlement money, Holly has enough to focus on college and her future. I think Holly has a right to leave this behind.

"WAIT. HOLLY DROPPED THE CHARGES?"

Detective Walbrook says Holly and her family thought it was best.

"These cases are always difficult on survivors and the family.
Sometimes survivors drop after they press charges because of stress.
Even you have the option of dropping if the case becomes too much."

This is why Holly ignored my messages.
Detective Walbrook's demeanor remains calm.
As if my chances of beating this case
haven't just taken a nosedive out the window.

"If it's worth anything at all,
I for one believe you have a really strong case.
But this is Holly's decision."

Says,

"There is nothing we can do."

NOTHING THEY CAN DO

If I knew I would ever hear Detective Walbrook say the words

there is nothing we can do

I would have said I made the whole thing up.

If I knew there was *nothing they could do*

I would have prepared myself for the disappointment.

If I knew there was *nothing they could do*

I would have stopped myself from crying.

Maybe by trying that eye-rolling thing I learned again—
but instead, I'm too late.

I'm crying into my own sleeves instead.

WORDS

All Detective Walbrook can offer me are kind words.
All my father offers Detective Walbrook are harsh words.

Words won't bring me justice.
Words won't guarantee my safety.

Words got me here in the first place
and if I chose not to say them,
I wouldn't be in this mess.

Maybe there's a reason I felt all alone.
As if nobody understood.
Holly was the only person who could have.

Now I know the truth is *nobody does*.

PLANS WITH TALIA

Amina: Hey Talia, do you have a minute?

Five hours later Talia says,

Talia: So sorry I'm just getting this!

Just got back from the mall with Julia!

Everything okay?

I say,

Amina: It's fine.

Knowing it's a lie.
But something in me doesn't want to lie anymore.
I say,

Amina: Just wanted to hang out.

It's been a while.

Two hours later Talia says,

Talia: It has! I'm sorry!

Let's have a sleepover!!

Like we used to!

I say,

Amina: Let's do it!

YOU HAVE TO GO TO THERAPY NOW
(SO YOU DON'T END UP SAD WHEN YOU GET OLDER)

is what my father says after reading one too many pamphlets
provided by my school's counseling office.

My father said my school counselors recommended a list of therapists.
(The same list they recommend to every other fucked-up kid.)

Therapy was never an option in my home.
Before today, my father would tell you that *prayer*
is the best therapy.

The way my father holds his feelings in, I didn't think he'd call.
Thought holding my feelings in
made me a daughter following her father's footsteps.

I tried telling him I didn't need one.
That I would even make honor roll to prove it.
But my father kept saying no. Probably because:

I have to go to therapy now. So I don't end up sad when I get older.

STUPID THERAPIST

The first therapist my father drove me to
practically looked my age.
Like one of those teachers at school
who is always being confused for a student.
Her hair was strawberry blond,
and she wore a pencil skirt
with uncomfortable toe-squeezing wedges.

After the first session she told my father
she "doesn't believe she's a good fit."
I'm not sure if it's because I didn't speak for most of session
or because when I did I asked when session would end.

Some therapist.

THERAPY OFFICES AND HOSPITALS

both have the smell of hand sanitizer floating in the air.

Emotional support posters plaster the walls.
The one above me is a poster about teen-dating violence,
but my favorite is the one that reads,
"Never Forget Your Re**spec**tables!"
with a photo of a man with glasses occupying half his face.

I fill out paperwork that asks the same question
twelve different ways. A thin older woman with light bright skin
and yellow tea-party heels walks into the lobby.

Her top is a horrible tie-dye attempt her grandchild probably created
and her skirt is flowy and floor length.
She looks around the room, confused,
as if it's her first time here too.

The woman calls for an Amina Conteh,
and I check both sides of me.

No way this woman is my therapist.

"AMINA CONTEH?"

She calls my name again and my father
gestures toward me.
I get up and follow her to her office.

Not only does she dress like a child, but her desk,
entirely covered in papers and office supplies,
looks like a child's too.

An old-looking brown leather sofa occupies half the room.
In front of the couch is a small black table and a candy bowl.
At least this therapist has good taste in chocolate.

I plop onto the couch without saying a word
while she looks through my paperwork.

She tells me to take a seat and get comfortable.

Too late.

INTAKE SESSION WITH DR. MILLER

After she's gotten all her papers together,
she tells me she knows a bit of what brings me to her
based on her conversation with my father and intake form.

She asks me what my personal goals for therapy are
and I shrug, because personally, my goal right now is to be home.

Dr. Miller asks me if everything is all right
and I still don't say anything.
Maybe if I go the whole session without responding
she'll run and tell my dad she doesn't
"think I'm a good fit" like the last one.

I almost feel bad,
if there's one thing I haven't been doing it's speaking.

The one thing I have been doing
is eating all the chocolate in her candy bowl.

Kit Kats taste better in therapy sessions you don't want to be in.

A NOTEPAD AND A PEN

After thirty minutes of wrestling with my silence
Dr. Miller offers a notepad and pen,
asking if I'd rather write how I'm feeling.

Says some people
"find therapy a bit easier if they write things down."

I take the notepad—still only sharing my silence.

I write:

April 9

I wish people knew

I STOP WRITING.

Realizing I am here
because *too many* people know things.
Things I never wanted to share.

My story became available for everyone's consumption.
Shared in police stations.
On pulpits.
In homes.
On the news.
Over coffee.

Made an example of.

April 9

~~I wish people knew~~ The truth is I wish people knew nothing about me at all.

Amina: Hey Holly, can we talk?

I don't want to get in your business or anything

but I spoke with Detective Walbrook and she told me.

Let me know when you get this?

APRIL 23: 111 DAYS UNTIL TRIAL

EVEN STICK-UP-HER-ASS HAMILTON FEELS BAD FOR ME.

In the last month, she has allowed me
three quiz resubmissions and "accidentally"
forgot to mark two of my wrong answers on the last.

Today during class, Bowl Cut mumbles under his breath
when I answer a question wrong:

"She's known for making up stories about people
and making up answers in class I guess."

Normally, I would have something slick to say
but I keep my mouth shut.
In a room where half the students
have heard rumors of me being the girl who got the
cookout-throwing,
community-loving,
job-providing pastor locked up,
what does anything I say matter?

I don't have the time, the energy, or the patience
to care about anything or anyone right now.

MS. HAMILTON HAD TIME TODAY

I may not have had the time, but Ms. Hamilton did.

"Disrespectful comments, even when whispered,
will not be tolerated in my class."

Bowl Cut stumbles over his own words
like a drunk stumbles over his own feet.

"It wasn't me!"

Like the amateur he is,
making himself a guilty party before he was indicted.

Hamilton shoots back:

"I don't believe I said it was you.
Speak with me after class."

I laugh in Ms. Hamilton's class for the first time.
I know what's about to happen when Ms. Hamilton says
Speak with me after class.

Someone is getting a phone call home.
But this time

it ain't me.

WHEN I GET HOME

I learn it actually *was me*.

I haven't received a positive phone call home
since the fourth grade when I won student of the month.

My father says,
"Something about you keeping your composure.
Says she's proud."

PROUD.

This is what finally makes someone proud of me.
For being too exhausted to speak back.

What reason does a girl have to fight anything
in a world that protects you only when you're silent?

MAY 7
10:27 A.M.

Katie Walbrook: Thank you for taking the time to speak with me again, Mr. Conteh. I know this process is long, but we're doing the best we can and this follow-up will really help us prepare the best possible case.

Nigel Conteh: Anything to help.

Katie Walbrook: So you and Amina have been active members of Holy Tabernacle for many years. You were inactive for several months about ten years ago, but after that were active until last January, am I correct?

Nigel Conteh: That is correct.

Katie Walbrook: How would you describe your relationship with Randall Johnson?

Nigel Conteh: He was someone people looked to for advice. After Amina's mom passed, he was so happy to invite us back to church. I thought he was someone we could trust.

Katie Walbrook: I can assure you, you are not the only person who believed Randall Johnson was someone who could be trusted. He had a lot of people fooled.

Nigel Conteh: I just want him to be held accountable for what he did.

Katie Walbrook: I understand, Mr. Conteh.

Nigel Conteh: I wish I never trusted him.

SLEEPOVER

Talia is the only friend my father has ever let spend the night.
When she comes in, they banter
and he congratulates her on her first straight-A report card.
He'll probably bring it up later this week
when he sees mine and the big fat C-
next to every class.

Except for Hamilton, who is giving me a B+
despite me retaking every single quiz until I stop failing.

Talia sees my closet,
which went from half full
to barely fitting all the clothes I have now.

She gives herself a tour.

"When did you buy all these outfits?!
And these shoes?! All without me?!"

She rummages through them.

"My dad gives me an allowance now,
so I took myself shopping."

Her eyes widen,
"Shopping? Without me?!"

The truth is,
I *wanted* to go with her.
But when I asked her what she was doing after school last week,
I heard the same name I hear every other time.

Julia.   *Julia.*   *Julia.*

UNO

It's tradition.

Whenever we hang out at each other's houses,
sometime throughout the night we make bets over Uno.
Usually for a couple of dollars, or a dare.
A couple of times we've bet homework assignments,
and sometimes we bet secrets.

The first time we ever played, years ago,
I learned Talia had never been kissed,
she learned I didn't know how to ride a bike.

We haven't made bets for secrets in years.
Why would we?
When we know everything there is to know already.

CAN I ASK YOU A QUESTION?

After two games of Uno, and learning
Talia sucked her thumb to fall asleep until she was eight and googled
"how to kiss" in preparation for her first date with Julia,

Talia says:

"Since it's clear I won't be winning anytime soon,
I'll cut to the chase—
Can I ask you a question?"

I don't respond before she says,

"Deon reached out to me a couple days ago.
He figured it out, Mina. He's really worried about you."

My mouth locks and my heart does that weird
fast pounding thing when you're caught in a lie,
or you eat too fast—
or when your best friend is about to ask a question
she should know better than to ask.

"He's really confused.
Maybe you can try to talk to him?"

NO PITY PARTIES

I know that Deon is not his uncle or his mother.

I don't want him to feel guilty about it,
even though he probably talked to Talia because he does.

Truth is, I don't want the pity.
The last thing I want is another complicated emotion to hold.

Reaching out to him will bring just that,
another emotion I do not want to feel.

THESE DAYS, I DON'T FEEL MUCH OF ANYTHING

It's as if my body is reacting in reverse.
Everything that would normally upset me,
now makes me feel nothing at all.

Like when your leg falls asleep,
except now I feel that all over my body.
Numb to the world around me,
except a gentle buzz,
the only reminder I am still alive.

I feel nothing whether my father is silent
or yelling at some prosecutor.

Nothing when Bowl Cut has trouble minding his own business.

Nothing when Deon tries to offer support.

THESE DAYS, I DON'T FEEL MUCH OF ANYTHING AT ALL— BUT NOT TODAY.

"Maybe you should have told him
if I wanted to speak to him I would.
I didn't tell him because I don't want to talk about it.
And I shouldn't have to."

Talia says,

"He really cares about you.
I remember how happy you were with him,
and you deserve that."

I don't care how much Deon cares about me.
I don't care if he is concerned.

What I care about is the fact that this is the first time
in weeks Talia has checked in with me,
and all because a boy told her he's concerned.

TIMES WHEN TALIA *SHOULD* HAVE BEEN CONCERNED:

- When I first reported and I asked her to come over, and she couldn't because she was shopping with Julia instead.
- When I called her three times when I was down, and she missed every single call.

This is the time she cares.

This is when she notices.

When she finally talks to me about anything
other than clothes,
or hair,
or shopping.

MAYBE IT'S NORMAL

Maybe it's normal to cry after someone calls out your sadness.
Maybe it's normal to cry when you and your best friend are fighting.

I don't know how I end up on the floor,
curled like a caterpillar,
swimming in a pool of my misery and tears.

Talia brings me tissues from my desk
and sits on the floor with me,
reminding me to breathe.
Between sobs, I say,

"You're only worried about me because Deon is."

Talia insists it's not because of Deon.
That she's worried about me too.

I'm not sure what has me more upset—
the fact that two people who are supposed to care about me the most
are having meetings to talk about their broken friend
or this argument ruining my first sleepover
with my best friend in months.

Talia tells me she didn't know how to bring it up.
She didn't want to make me "even more stressed."

I breathe.
Like breathing is the only thing I know how to do.

IN THE MIDDLE OF MY SOBBING

I get a text from Deon.

Deon: Hey Mina, if you're free,

I was thinking on Saturday we could hang out?

Maybe we could go to the Harbor or The Shack?

Do one of those puzzles you like?

As much as Talia pretends she didn't see the message,
I know she did.

I tell her she should go.

She tells me,

"It's okay to not know what you want.
Sometimes telling someone where you're at
can help them know what *not* to do."

It's not that Talia cares too little
or that Deon cares too much.
It's that I don't know how to care for myself.

I say I want to be left alone,
to which Talia responds:

"Look, you don't have to text Deon back.
But we both really want you to be okay."

I shout,

"Talia, I said I want to be left alone!"

Talia and I have never even raised our voices at each other.
But here I am,
yelling at my best friend.

"First you come over and run straight to my clothes,
now you're more concerned with Deon than me!
Maybe you should be hanging out with him!
Or Julia, since she's all you even care about now!"

Talia looks at me.
As shocked to hear me yelling at her,
as I am to realize I actually did.
Before she grabs her things, she says:

"I know it's hard but what you're doing
is so important for other people out there,
and people want to support you through it."

I want to tell Talia,

I never wanted to be the back that carries a movement.
Never wanted to be the megaphone
that amplifies the survivor's song.

All I wanted was a listening ear,
willing to understand my story for what it is,
and not what people think it should be.

Someone willing to hear my story,
and love me,

Anyway.

IN THERAPY

Dr. Miller has been trying to get me to talk more.

Every single time she asks me about my day,
I tell her that it's been the same as every other day.
Why would I talk about my week every session,
when every week sounds like a bad remix?

Talia and I haven't spoken in eleven days.
And I've ignored Deon so many times,
even if I did try to talk to him,
he probably wouldn't want to now.

When I tell Dr. Miller this,
she asks me how often I journal.

I tell her I haven't journaled since that night
and before then I only did at Holy Tabernacle,
the place I want nothing to do with.

Dr. Miller says it may help me open up
in a way speaking won't allow.

For fifteen minutes,
she asks me to write how I feel in this moment.

I write:

May 19

I don't understand how tragedy can change all the things you once cherished.

Talia and I don't speak. Before we'd never gone more than a day without speaking. Even at lunch, she's been sitting with Julia now instead of me.

I know Deon wants to understand, but I don't know how to talk to him about it. I don't know how to talk about all the complicated emotions. The same parts of me I wanted so badly to share with him were violated by a man we both trusted.

My father and I still don't say much. It's awkward building a relationship we both know probably wouldn't exist if something bad hadn't happened.

I don't have anyone. I don't have anything.

I've always been ready for battle, but for the first time, I'm losing an entire war and I'm not sure if I'll ever be victorious again.

HEROIC SUPER GIRL

Dr. Miller spends the rest of our session
trying to convince me I am some type of heroic super girl.
That so many women in my community are looking up to me

It's a bit ironic—
the sight of his face makes me gag.
The "community's" sight of his face
still gets their support in the comment sections.

When I tell her this,
she assures me my emotions are normal
and welcome in this space.

I don't believe her,
but for the first time,
I *want* to.

SHE GETS IT

> **Holly:** Hey Amina, sorry I'm responding late.

> How about The Shack this Saturday at 5?

> Can we keep this between you and me please?

> My parents won't know I'll be coming.

Sometimes you need to hear from someone
who gets what you're going through.

Sometimes you want to hear everything will be okay
from someone who's going through something *with* you.
Instead of someone who's rooting for you from the outside looking in.

I don't blame Holly for leaving me on read for so long,
because I know Holly and I will probably never be best friends
and I don't blame her—

But friends or not friends,
she is the only person who was a part of this case with me.

Maybe Holly dropped charges
because she needs to be convinced we can get through this.
Together.

> **Amina:** Perfect and your secret is safe with me.

> I won't tell anyone. See you Saturday!

MAY 28: 76 DAYS UNTIL TRIAL

A HUSTLER'S SPRING

A Baltimore spring is a hustler's season.

After a long winter being cooped in the house,
neighborhood kids come out to play, selling snow cones
on the sidewalk for a quick dollar.

Squeegee boys walking up and down the streets,
trying to clean windshields for a quick tip.

Musicians come out of hiding to perform at the Harbor.
Some of the best saxophone players on the East Coast,
they alone have enough talent to carry a whole new renaissance.

Hustlin' is a part of a Baltimorean's blood.
Because we know how to get by.
Because we have to.
Because nobody will look out for us
the way we can.

NERVES

My father drops me off at The Shack
and says he'll be eating dinner at a restaurant a few blocks away.
I don't tell him Holly and I are meeting.

Instead, he believes Talia and I are,
and he doesn't ask me any questions:

His depressed daughter is *finally* being social again.

So far, I've fidgeted with my own fingers,
   the napkin holder
   & a saltshaker

I shake salt onto the table,
until Mr. Richard walks over.

"You holding up all right, Mina?"

I nod

"Yes," I lie.

5:10 P.M.

The time is now 5:10,
which means Holly and I are were supposed to meet ten minutes ago,
and coincidently, every five-four girl
with light brown skin and coily hair
who walks into the restaurant looks like her.

I grab my phone, text Holly:

Amina: Hey, everything okay?

I'm waiting for you at The Shack at a table

on the left-hand side when you get here.

5:27 P.M.

At 5:27 Holly walks in and sits at the table,
her voice carrying less life than usual when she says:

"Hello."

This time, she doesn't have questions.
She isn't eager to see me,
the way I was to see her.

I wave, a grin plastered on my face from cheek to cheek.
Only to hear her say,

"I'm only here because you won't stop bugging me.
If you want me to press charges again,
spit it out. Because I won't.
And I won't have the conversation twice."

THEY BELIEVED IT WOULD BE BEST

Holly tells me she told her parents
it would be best to drop criminal charges
after Holy Tabernacle offered a settlement,
and they agreed.

Says she and her family believed it would be best
to toss this whole mess behind them
and use the money to start fresh in suburbia.

Says she's afraid to fight in a system that constantly
proves it is designed for us to lose.

Asks,

"Do you remember my brother, Jonathan?"

ALMOST AS HOLY—ALMOST

Jonathan was *almost* as holy as Holly.
Always volunteering and shit.
Until high school.

I don't remember much about him,
I know he went to some fancy boarding school in PG County,
and he barely comes back to Baltimore anymore.

I remember always hearing his name out of somebody's mouth
for being "a fresh young thing."
I don't tell Holly that.
I tell her,

"I don't remember much."

THE WORDS NOBODY WANTS TO HEAR

Holly tells me her brother and her parents pressed charges
after a sexual misconduct incident with a high school teacher.

Except, unlike Holly, her brother never dropped charges.
He went to all the court prep dates,
suffered all the high school gossip,
only to experience the nightmare every survivor fears.

Having your day in court,
mustering all the courage you've struggled
to scrape together during the past year,
convincing yourself you will finally
receive the justice you deserve,
staring a jury right in the face,
only to hear the words:

Not Guilty.

FORWARD

Holly says Johnson got close to their family
by offering them prayers,
                              inspirational phone calls,
                              private Bible studies at their home.

Says she originally didn't want to press charges.
& if she hadn't talked to Jonathan about it,
who then talked to her parents,
she probably never would have.

After what happened with her brother,
her parents told her the decision was hers.

So in the beginning, she chose to fight.

"I did the one thing I've been afraid of.
Went to a police station, pressed charges,
only to have all the parts of my life that scare me
broadcasted all over the internet."

Says she lost her will to fight.

When her family got the settlement money,
her parents told her they have enough to start over.
Pretend this never happened.

I ask her,

"Don't you want to know you tried?"

And she shoots back,

"I did."

Says,

"You call it giving up,
                              but I call it moving forward."

NOBODY GETS IT

I thought Holly would be the first person
to make me feel seen since walking into that police station.

The first person who would understand me
since that night in the church office.

Talia will never truly get it.
Deon will never truly get it.
My father will never truly get it.

I should have known better
than to assume I would be understood.

How can I expect to be seen
when every single day,
I can barely even recognize myself?

ON TIME (FOR ONCE)

Dad: Finished? My dinner just ended.

On my way to pick you up now.

Maybe my father being on time to pick me up for once
is the first blessing I've received in months.
Like God's saying "sorry" for the shit show my life's become.

Holly will not change her mind.

My heart sinks, realizing without Holly,
I truly am in this by myself.

I tell her I've felt so alone,
and I know she probably does too.
That at least before, we were in this together.
Holly says,
"In this together?"

Holly's voice is cold when she says it.
She continues,

"We were never in this together.
We weren't in this together when you were calling
me Holy Holly behind my back thinking I never knew.
We weren't in this together when I sent
all those messages you didn't respond—"

Holly stops speaking for a moment.
A look of fear flushes her face.

I DIDN'T KNOW

"Did you know he would be here?!"

Outside the window, I see my father's car parked.
But it's not just my father I see.

He is arguing with a man Holly recognizes before I do.

Johnson.

She looks at me, a rage in her eyes,

"This is why my family and I moved away!
The first time I come here, this happens?"

I want to say,

I swear I didn't know he would be here.
I don't want to see him any more than you do.

But all my words get stuck in my throat like a lump of clay.
& before I can find them again,
Holly is already walking to her car.

I follow her,
and my father is standing right in front of me
with his hand in Johnson's face.

Yelling,

"I can't tell you how many times I wanted to kill you.
You're lucky I don't want to spend my next years in prison,
rotting there like you will!"

The first time I have ever seen him say he would kill someone.
The first time I have ever worried my father will keep his word.

I see Johnson. Standing there. Stammering.

The whole restaurant is staring through the windows,
and for the first time,
I see Johnson looking unsure of himself.

"Mr. Conteh—I can explain this."

Mr. Richard hears what's happening
and rushes out of The Shack yelling,

"You don't have to explain anything!
Explain it in court and to your future fellow inmates.
The whole community knows what you did to those girls,
so I suggest you take your ass away from my shack!"

MY MOMENT

Holly will probably never trust me again.

       Talia will probably never be my friend again.

              Deon will probably never date me again.

And I am standing in front of the cause.

This is my moment.

When I can finally do what I wish I did that night in his office.
Look Johnson straight in the face and stand up for myself.

I look Johnson right in his face,
my voice quiet, but firm.

"We all know what you did."

I take a step closer,
my hands and mouth shaking,
but my legs carry me.

"YOU know what you did—"

MY MOMENT—INTERRUPTED

My father tells me to get in the car.
Let grown people do what grown people do,
but even in the midst of my own fear,
I can't help but shout.

"You're the reason my entire life fell apart!
And I couldn't speak then, but I'm here to speak now—"

My father yells again,
this time, at me.

"Amina, please! Get in the car!
I said we'll handle this!"

I tell my father this is nobody's business but mine.
That this is my chance to do what I wish I did.

Only Johnson is already running toward his car.
Fleeing from all responsibility,
once again.

SHOULD HAVE MINDED YOUR OWN BUSINESS

During the car ride home,
my father and I sit in silence.

We do not speak about what happened.
We do not listen to my father's *Singers of Praise: Live!* CD.

The car remains quiet,
and I say:

"You should have minded your business back there.
The way you always have minded your business
with everything else that happens to me."

EXCUSE ME?

"Excuse me, young lady?"

I know I shouldn't be speaking to my father this way.
But it's true.

For the first time in so long,
I wanted to *say something*.

Even if I didn't have the right words.

Even if my voice would shake.

I finally started to find the power to speak up.

My father stole that from me.

ANYWHERE BUT HERE

"I said, you should have let me handle my own shit!
The way I always have!"

My father has never heard me curse.
Even when he's heard me say the word *hell*,
I talked about the biblical place.

I know cursing at him isn't right.
But *I don't care.*

I tell my father I need to breathe,
get out the car at the stoplight,
start running in the opposite direction of home.

"And where do you think you're going?!"

I don't even turn around when I shout my answer:

"Anywhere but fucking here!"

I AM IN NEED OF A MIRACLE

There are only two people I know of
who could make this better.
One wants nothing to do with a horrible best friend,
the other I've spent months ignoring.

When I am far enough from my father's car,
I catch my breath, pull out my phone, text:

Amina: Hey Deon, I know I've been distant and I'm really sorry for that,

but could you pick me up? At the park by my house.

I could really use the company.

In less than two minutes, he responds:

Deon: Of course.

DEON TO THE RESCUE

Missed Calls: Dad (3)

I meet Deon at the park we used to sneak off to.

He is wearing a yellow sweatshirt—
A color I love, and he hates.
He looks almost as nervous as I do,
drumming his thumbs against the steering wheel.

"You like my shirt?"

He pops his nonexistent T-shirt collar.
Says,

"I figured I could look ridiculous if there's a chance you'd smile.
My sweatshirt kinda match your highlights.
They look great by the way."
He pauses before he continues.

"I haven't hung out with you in so long,
I never got the chance to tell you."

I want to smile, but I don't.
Can't.

My hands are still shaking from seeing Johnson,
and my throat is still sore from shouting at my father.

THERE'S HOPE

Perhaps it was the silent tears I've tried to wipe away,
or the fact that I haven't stopped rocking back
and forth since I got in the car,
but after ten minutes riding in silence,
Deon says:

"Mina, I know things have been hard for you lately.
And I want you to know that I love that you're my girl—
actually. Can I still call you my girl?"

He smiles, and for the first time I do too.

Says,
"But you know I'm your friend first, right?"

And I know, not everything has changed like I worried.

I'M SAFE

Missed Calls: Dad (7)

After an hour of riding aimlessly around the city,
my phone buzzes with the seventh missed call from my father.

Deon says:

"Your dad's sure been calling you a lot.
Don't you want to get that?"

I shake my head.
I know I should pick up the phone,
I know my father is worried about me.
But he's the last person I want to hear from.
So I let the phone
Ring
Ring
Ring.

Missed Calls: Dad (10)

Deon says:

"Listen, I won't keep pressing.
But at least text him and let him know you're safe."

I pull out my phone, text my father just that,
nothing more.

Amina: I'm safe.

WHAT I WANT

Being with Deon for the first time in months
is more nerve-racking than a first date.

We've gone through all the surface conversations.
School,
music,
even the weather.

The gears in my brain won't stop
replaying what happened at The Shack.

Holly never trusting me again,
my dad hurting my feelings,
me hurting his.

One of the last things Talia said to me when we fought
is sometimes you don't know what you want.

In this moment, I know exactly what I want.
I know I want my best friend back,
and though she probably wants nothing to do with me,
I pull out my phone, text:

Amina: I'm sorry.

You're my best friend and I don't want to lose that.

Can we talk this through?

Getting my best friend back is one thing I want.
The next requires me to use my words.
I look toward Deon,
voice shaking, ask:

"Is it okay if I hold your hand?"

He grabs mine before saying,

"I don't know the last time you asked me
if you could hold my hand. They might be sweaty,
but if you promise not to hate me for that, then sure."

I laugh,
for the first time in a long time,
assure him I'll take him for his sweaty hands,
as long as he doesn't mind taking me for mine.

DEON DOESN'T HAVE TO ASK MANY QUESTIONS

He has a way of letting me know he'll be there
for the moments when I do want to talk,
and he'll stay there during the moments when I don't.

He cracks jokes about how boring his history class has been,
his brother's messy car,
even jokes about his grandma-approved style of driving.

Whatever he thinks will make me smile.

He says:

"Maybe we should grab something to eat?"

With everything going down,
I didn't realize I never ate my food at The Shack.

I don't know how he does it,
but he always knows exactly what I need.

CATCHING UP

Deon picks up tacos from our favorite takeout spot
and parks the car while we eat.
(Mid-bite) he says:

"Can I ask how you're doing?
Been a while since we've talked."

I say:

"It's been hard.
After everything happened,
I didn't want to be around anyone."

He says:

"Me, your dad, Talia,
we all care about you.
We always will."

I say:

"You care about me.
But do you believe me?"

Without pause, he says:

"Yes. I promise,
I've always been on your side."

I say:

"But did you always believe Holly?
You said your mom didn't.
Did you even disagree?"

He says:

"I'M SORRY"

"That was a hard time. My mom took longer
to process than she should have. We've talked about it since then.
I promise you I believed Holly before I even knew it was Holly.
And I have *always* believed you."

I cry so bad,
my face puffs up and a headache's coming on.

Deon hugs me and says,

"Everything is okay.
Everything will work out."

He continues,

"I want you to know if I had to choose
between him and protecting you,
I would protect you every time, without a doubt.
You're who I care about.
You're the person I will choose,
again and again."

He doesn't let go as he tells me what happened wasn't my fault,
and the people around you
are there to hold you up when you can't hold yourself.

He says all he can say,
and when he runs out of words,
he continues to hold me.

Holds me until I can hold myself.

MY FOUR-LEAF CLOVER

Maybe Deon is a good luck charm,
like a four-leaf clover or rabbit's foot in human form.
Because when he begins to drive me home,
I get a message:

Talia: I'm sorry too.

I know we can work this out.

I meant it when I said people want

to see you happy you know.

I tell Deon:

"You know, I'm learning the people who love you
are always right when it matters."

Amina: I know. Thanks Talia.

Also, I can't get into it now,

but you were right about Deon.

Talia responds.
This is the first time I have ever loved reading the words:

Talia: Girl, I told you so.

DEON'S HAND

I reach for Deon's hand.

For the rest of the drive,
we laugh.
Making up for all the time lost.

We even listen to an R&B station, which,
considering what happened the last night we listened,
will always prompt a laugh between us.

"Deon?"

I say as he parks the car.

"Yeah, Mina?"

I grab my bag and get ready to head to my house.

"Thank you for being my friend first."

He tells me he wouldn't trade it for anything,
and as he begins to tell me how much he enjoyed our night—

I KISS HIM

For the first time since all this,
I kiss Deon
(and while I'll never get to say we had sex in his brother's car),
it's good.

So I kiss him

>   again,

>   and again.

& that's what I want;
(maybe even need) in this exact moment.

I need someone to let me know everything is okay.
To hold me,
and someone to hold.

Who better than someone who loves you,
who you love too?

He looks at me, smiles, and says,

"I'm really glad you texted me, Mina."

TROUBLE AT HOME (AT HOME IN TROUBLE)

I walk through my apartment door,
and my father is sitting at the dining room table.

My father and I haven't been to a Sunday service in months,
but I know a prayer in someone's eyes when I see one,
and I know a prayer in my heart when I feel it too.

I want everything to be okay.
But tonight's damage is irreparable.

Normally if something like this happened before,
I would be worried about the repercussions.
    Not being able to leave the house until I'm thirty,
    getting my phone taken away.

Shit, after what I pulled tonight,
I should be worried about getting my *life* taken away.

I always felt I could not hold anger toward my father
because he holds a roof over my head.

But today, I had a chance to speak,
and he took that from me.

The silence in the room is so loud
until my father says:

"I wanted to stay up to make sure you were safe.
We will address tonight another day. Head to your room."

MIRACLE MESSES

They say the best miracles are made of messes.

It's been one week since my father and I ran into Johnson,
and the silence in our home has grown even louder.

Every day I would come home
and wish he would say something.

I used to wish he could see me for more than an invisible girl

that he would say something *to* me
but every day looks the same.

Come home	Go to room	Lock my door
Do my homework	Mind my business	Get to bed
Avoid my father	Avoid my father	Avoid my father

A BIRTHRIGHT

When I was younger, my mother would start each week by asking:

"What miracles would you like to make today?"

Because my mother believed in a God
but still, knew she was a Goddess too.

Believed in all things all powerful
while still knowing, for some women,
making our own miracles is as much a responsibility
as it is a birthright.

IF MY MOTHER WAS ALIVE

she would have taken charge.

She wouldn't have asked questions,
the way my father did when he first learned.

She would have raised her voice and her fist—
in the air and straight to Johnson's nose—
the way he deserved.

She would have made a miracle.
She wouldn't have waited for one.

I want to be my own Goddess,
but I don't know how to make my own miracles.

How do you make miracles
when your life has turned into a tragedy?

When the miracle I've always wanted
was a mother who would fight for me.
A father who speaks *to* me.

But instead,
my father chooses to be silent
and speak only when it's *over* me.

JUNE 17: 56 DAYS UNTIL TRIAL

JOINT THERAPY SESSION

After I tell Dr. Miller about what happened at The Shack,
she suggests my father join us for a therapy session.

She says she's used joint therapy in similar situations
and found it's always "beneficial."

I try telling her there's no use.

I bet none of those "similar situations" included a father
who chose to ignore his child's existence their whole life.

None of those situations included a father
who stole his daughter's voice the one time it mattered to her.

Even a miracle conjured by God himself couldn't fix it,
so why does she believe we can during our little sessions?

Dr. Miller told me to "give it a chance."
I tell her I have nothing to say to him.

She tells me:

"Well, good thing you can always listen."

THE WAY HE RAISED ME

I walk into the session determined to be as silent
as my father raised me to be.

My father follows. If it wasn't clear to Dr. Miller,
it should be clear now, where I learned silence.

He gives her one-word answers.
"Yes" and "No" to every question she asks.

Dr. Miller might be patient,
but I certainly am not.

"This is all he does. Stays silent
during the times when it actually matters."

As soon as those words left my mouth,
I knew I'd made a mistake.

My father looks hurt
but still continues to give half-assed answers.

DR. MILLER SAYS

"Amina's told me a bit about her mother during past sessions.
Can you tell me about your relationship with her?"

My father and I never really speak about my mom
and I've only spoken about her with Dr. Miller a couple times.

So, I'm surprised
when she asks him if he sees any similarities between me and her.
He says he sees her in me so much it makes him afraid.
Says:

"I always said I would tell you but I always found a reason not to.
Maybe because I knew it would be hard for me.
But after everything that has happened, I think it is overdue."

THE TRUTH

My father says seeing me hurt
reminds him of the way my mother used to hurt
whenever anyone stood in the way of her doing what's right.

"There are so many stories I've always intended to share with you.
The silly faces she used to make,
the way she used to dance around the home to her favorite songs."

My father says when my mom passed,
those memories became painful to hold.
Like he was dreaming of someone he knew would never return.
That his heart couldn't handle it.

Dr. Miller reaches for a box of tissues,
and my father begins crying before he says,

"One day you saw your mother leave for a summer to visit home,
and in a matter of a couple weeks, we lost her.
The only way I knew how to explain her death was to tell you
she lost her life in an accidental fire."

A PARTIAL TRUTH

I always knew my mother was unafraid to speak up.
What I didn't know was *how much* she spoke.

My father says what he told me about her death is only partially true.
Says,

"At her core she was a freedom fighter.
Your mother was a victim of a fire believed to be purposeful."

ALL THE FIGHTING PARTS

I've always thought of myself   as the mirror of my mother

Always thought all   the fighting parts of me

            were inherited from her.

But when I see my father   speaking about his loss, I see

the way he fought. & I believe   I inherited my fighting parts

            from him too.

THE MAP

The loss of my mother
was the biggest loss
my family has ever known.

When we lost her,
we lost ourselves
we lost each other.

Today, with my father & Dr. Miller
I find myself,

ready   to   (re)draw   the   map.

QUESTIONS

Soon, Dr. Miller has to offer us both tissues,
when my father holds my hand and I begin crying too.

I want to know everything.

What was she fighting for?

Why would anyone hate her cause enough to take her life?

Why my mom's?

I must wear my questions on my face,
because before I can ask,
my father continues,

"She wanted to visit family in our village back home.
She was supposed to come back to us at the end of the summer."

I remember when I was younger,
my mother said she would be spending a summer in Sierra Leone,
& I cried the whole night through.

But even as a kid,
you know the summer is long—but never lasts forever.

I knew in my heart she would be coming back,
until the one day I learned she wouldn't.
Couldn't.

My father,
voice shaking,
hands fidgeting,
says,

"Shortly after your mother left,
there began what would later become a war back home.
The ramifications led to the deaths of over fifty thousand people.
Including your mother."

THE MISSING PUZZLE PIECE

My father says my mother's heart always belonged to home.
The only place that ever felt more home to her,
other than Sierra Leone,
was the one she built in Baltimore
with us.

"She promised that at the end of the summer she would come back,
but when children from her village
got recruited as child soldiers during the war,
her heart didn't allow her to leave. Her heart told her to fight."

I've heard stories of the war.
I've heard of how the need for power can make a monster.

What I didn't know was how that monster took my mother's life.

THE STORY GOES

My mother stayed.
She fought.

She wrote letters, she protested.
She used her voice,
to speak for young people who couldn't use theirs.

She promised she was going to leave if it ever got too bad,
but the week before she was supposed to return,
she attended her last protest and a flame engulfed her body,
along with seventeen other protestors.

I don't remember much of my mother,
but that's the thing about losing someone you love.

After you lose them,
you realize that the best way to continue to love them
is to honor the life they lived.

I cling to my father's every word.
Hear the stories of my mother my heart always yearned for.

"When your mother lost her life,
a case was filed to find the people at fault.
After several years, the case was dismissed.
They could never prove who was responsible.
The only thing safe to assume is it was a result
of what your mother and so many others fought for."

Though I've always fought with my words,
hearing my father tell my mother's story
makes me realize, even through his silence,
he's been fighting too.

And though I'm crying,
and I wonder how anyone
can harvest so much hate in their heart—

And although I am sad,
somehow, I'm not angry.
I'm proud.

My mother was a fighter.

I am proud to be the daughter
of a woman who fought.

ROAD TO FORGIVENESS

My father's silence makes sense.

It's not that he resents my mother,
he resents how people treated her when she spoke.

It's not that he resents me or even Detective Walbrook,
he is afraid of how people will treat me when I speak.

I don't know when I'll forgive him, but I can say,
if forgiveness were a road, *we're on it*.

I know forgiveness requires time.
But I know I can start by offering my own apology.

I tell my father I'm sorry about the other night at The Shack.

That I know it wasn't right of me,
and now that I know what happened with my mother,
at the very least I can understand where he's coming from.

I ask my father:

"I know it's hard to talk about,
but maybe you can tell me more stories of her?"

My father nods yes.
We hug.
For what is probably the first time in months.

My father is not a perfect man,
but he's human,
and for this I will love him always.

JUNE 28: 45 DAYS UNTIL TRIAL

BIRTHDAY COUNTDOWN BEGINS

"Your birthday is a month before your trial.
Anything you want to do to get your mind off things?"

Every conversation between Talia and me has been cut and dry.
Like we both know there's a giant unspoken-for elephant in the room.

"I don't know. I haven't really been too excited about it.
I've been thinking more about not receiving a guilty verdict.
I've been trying to prepare myself for the worst, you know?"

I've read all the resources,
attended all the court date prep meetings,
even practiced my testimony in the mirror,
like it's some sort of show,
and not the most desperate plea I carry.

NOBODY PREPARES YOU

When I first pressed charges,
nobody prepared me for the pressure.
About the lens I would be under.

The weight that comes with having something to prove
to people who are determined to make you small.
The pressure shows up at the most inopportune times.

Like the time I went on social media
and saw that a girl from Holy Tabernacle had written,
"Church hasn't felt the same without my pastor."

Or the time Talia and I drove home from the mall
and passed Holy Tabernacle on the way
& for a moment, the world seemed to blur.

Nobody warns you about how the mention
of their name makes your whole entire body
fold like a question mark:

How can the holiest of places break a person?

TALIA BRINGS ME BACK TO EARTH

Talia says,

"Well, I can tell you it doesn't matter
whether there's a guilty verdict or not.
And a judge,
jury,
or internet troll
can't change that."

And I nod.
I ain't sure I believe in a God,
but it felt a lot like saying,

Amen.

POLICE INTERVIEW TRANSCRIPT: JASMINE MILLER

JUNE 30
10:37 A.M.

Katie Walbrook: Thank you so much for meeting with me, Dr. Miller.

Jasmine Miller: My pleasure. When Amina mentioned that I might be contacted for an interview I was more than willing to help. I'm happy to assist with Amina's case.

Katie Walbrook: It's greatly appreciated. So I understand that you have been working with Amina in therapy sessions. Can you tell me how long you've been working with her?

Jasmine Miller: I've been working with Amina for about three months now. Her father brought her to our office in the beginning of April.

Katie Walbrook: Ah, I understand. For the record, do you mind telling us why you've been working with Amina?

Jasmine Miller: Of course. Amina and I began working together after she reported her sexual assault at the hands of Randall Johnson. We have been working together to address and confront the trauma she experienced during and after that event.

Katie Walbrook: And can you tell me a bit about your experience working with Amina?

Jasmine Miller: Amina has been making progress, but it's clear to me that she was heavily affected by the event.

Katie Walbrook: I see. And can you tell me a little bit about how exactly she was affected?

Jasmine Miller: She was unresponsive, was often teary-eyed, and up until fairly recently, was unable to communicate many of the feelings she was forced to confront because of Randall Johnson.

Katie Walbrook: Now that she communicates more, would you say that she's making substantial progress?

Jasmine Miller: Absolutely. And while that doesn't mean that she doesn't still experience the effects of that trauma, it does mean that she's learning the proper tools to identify and address what it is that she's feeling.

Katie Walbrook: I see. Thank you so much for taking the time to meet with me today.

Jasmine Miller: Absolutely anything I can do to help. What that man did is not right. I hope things work out in her favor.

Katie Walbrook: You and I both.

TRIAL IS THIRTY-SIX DAYS AWAY

So Dr. Miller and I dedicate sessions to preparing.

We've talked about all the fears I have,
tips for remaining calm when I take the stand,
about how a verdict doesn't determine what happened that night.

Lately I've been getting some parts of my life back.
But I can't help but think about the one thing I still don't understand.
Dr. Miller asks me if there's something on my mind I need to share.
I tell her:

"I met with Holly. The other survivor in the case.
She dropped the charges. I still don't know why
she would do that after everything we've been through."

Dr. Miller does that thing she always does,
when she exhales and goes *hmm*
while looking at the corner of the room.

"Have you ever thought that's why she would choose to drop?
Because of everything she's been through?"

HOLLY'S SHOES

"Holly's feelings aren't strange,
and neither are yours.
We're here for you to help you get through this."

Dr. Miller tells me she has a resource she wants us to review.
Another paper to read,
as if I didn't spend seven hours in school doing that.

"I know this is hard, Amina,
but it might be worth it to see things from Holly's perspective.
Try to place yourself in someone else's shoes."

WHILE READING

I learn for every 1,000 people
who are sexually assaulted, only 310 report.

Dr. Miller says,

"You've chosen your voice as your power.
You should be proud.
But try to understand you're in the minority.
Not everyone finds the courage to report,
but either way, you both will heal."

We dedicate the last ten minutes of the session to journaling.
I write:

July 7

I want to hate that Holly left me to fight this case on my own, but I don't think I ever will.

Truth be told, she's doing what I did. She's hiding from a world quicker to judge a girl than love on her. As much as the girl I was a year ago would only hate on Holly, the girl I am now can't help but understand her.

Holly and I are two girls with a story on display for our entire world to see. Girls who are both broken sometimes, trying to heal. Only difference is, for me, I chose for this case to be a part of that.

Nothing in this world can make me give up. Not when I've come this far. Not when I have something to prove. Not something to prove to Talia, to Deon, my father, my therapist, the local news stations, a judge, a jury, Holy Tabernacle, or even Johnson.

I got a grit and gall to me I will do everything to prove.

All for my damn self.

There is so much they don't tell you about surviving. You are a survivor because you overcame what tried to destroy you.

Maybe I am a survivor simply because I met fear, stared him right in the face, and chose to live anyway.

Amina: Hey, how are you?

I know it's been a wild time in both our lives.

I wanted to tell you you're on my mind

and I hope you're okay.

BIRTHDAY PLANS BUSTED

Every year on my birthday,
Talia makes a bigger deal of it than I ever would.

This year is no different.

According to her, a hard year requires a grand celebration.
Last week I found out Talia was *trying* to throw me a party
after Deon accidentally texted me:

> **Deon:** What day were you thinking for Mina's party again?

Followed by:

> **Deon:** Oh shit.

FRIDAY NIGHT

I spent days convincing Talia and Deon
inviting half my school to someone's cramped basement,
while someone passes out on the couch after two drinks,
isn't appealing.

Whether it's been a hard year or not.

I would rather have a night in
with people I care about most in the world.

After I finally convince them I'm not just *saying*
I don't want a party,
they both promise me they won't throw one.

After convincing my father Deon is a boy friend,
and not a boyfriend, he finally caved
and this Friday Talia and Deon are coming over for a movie night.

My father and I have been doing a lot better,
but I'm sure that would change if he learned Friday
won't be the first time Deon's been in his home.

Since Deon and I made up, we've had a lot of catching up to do
and most of that catching up happens in my room,
when my father's not home,
in my bed.

THE MELTING POT

is one of those fancy restaurants
where you have to cook the food yourself.
I've never understood paying extra to cook my own food,
but it was my mother's favorite.

My father is taking me to the Melting Pot
before Talia and Deon are supposed to come over.

My mother used to force my father and me to dress all fancy
and go there for dinner every month. But after she passed,
my father's money got tighter and we haven't been since.

Today, my mother isn't coming
but we still dress fancy, as if she's still with us.

SHE USED TO LOVE BIRTHDAYS

Today, on my seventeenth birthday,
my father and I sit on opposite sides of a booth.
The conversation half as empty as I remember since last being here.
Until he looks at me and says,

"You know, your mother used to love birthdays."

On the very few days when my father does speak about my mother,
the words usually come in the form of fragmented memories.

I nod and say:

"I actually remember that.
She used to sing happy birthday at the top of her lungs at midnight,
whether I was asleep or awake. Right?"

My father nods,
plays with his silverware.
I'm still shuffling responses in my head.

"From a young age, you have always taken after her.
Always willing to stand up for what you believe in.
That's why I fell for her, you know."

My father begins to clear his throat after choking on his words.
Our food is brought to us before he continues,

"That all is to say, you've battled with one hell of a year.
And you still manage to always fight back.
I know your mother is proud."

ON THE WAY HOME

all I think about is my mother.
How she actually *would* be proud.

For standing up for myself.
For learning how to create my own miracle.

While we drive home,
my father says:

"You know, I've really had trouble with the guilt.
I don't know how I let this happen.
How I believed he was a good man.
Sometimes I think if I was smarter,
none of this would have happened."

That's the thing about guilt.
When the innocent party experiences it,
you start apologizing for everything the guilty party did.
For all the ways they broke you.

My father isn't guilty here.
And neither am I.

My father has made his mistakes.
And we have a lot of work to do,
but we've been doing that.

FINALLY HOME

As we finally reach home, I look to my father.
I haven't been able to say much tonight,
but the three words I can say are

"I love you."

"SURPRISE!"

is what I hear when I walk through my front door,
and while I do hate surprises,
seeing my favorite people in corny birthday hats,
and a living room decked in streamers and decorations
(executed by Talia, I can tell)
might be the exception.

I may have said time and time again,
I didn't want a "party,"
but this is *exactly* what I needed.

My father looks at me smiling and gives me a hug
before he says,

"I'll let you teens do what teens do.
Enjoy your special day,
Mina."

TALIA SNEAKS ALCOHOL INTO MY FATHER'S HOME

After a few hours of binge-watching reality TV shows,
stuffing snacks in our faces,
and sneaking shots of liquor from Talia's bag,
Deon tells me they have more surprises.

Talia grabs a wrapped box from her bag.

"It's from the both of us," Talia says.

Deon chimes in and laughs while he says,

"Yeah, but only if you love it. If you hate it?
It was all Talia's idea."

Inside the box:
a leather journal with my name
a pen, engraved, that reads:

Mina,
With this may you shine a light.

THE GREATEST GIFT

Talia says:

"We already know you've been journaling lately
and we thought you should be doing so in style!"

Deon adds:

"Yeah, we're both really proud of you, Mina."

Before I can even say thank you, tears fall.

This isn't the first time this has happened—
me crying I mean.
It's a norm these days.

But this is the first time I've cried filled with joy
instead of sadness,
because I know the people around me love me,
because I know I'll always love them too.

THE THING ABOUT MIRACLES IS

Sometimes you don't have to create them.

Maybe the community you choose,
who love you enough to lift you up,
are your miracle.

And even though I didn't create
any miracles myself tonight,
I am still just as blessed.

THANKFUL

My father walks out the kitchen,
chocolate cake with yellow icing in hand.

Talia, Deon & I become actors,
painting on a sober face so good
my father thinks we're just "excited" about my birthday.

When Talia & Deon used all that "excitement"
and belted happy birthday to me,
my father sang right along with them.

The three people I love the most,

Happy birthday to you,
Happy birthday to you,
Happy birthday dear Mina,
Happy birthday to you.

JULY 23: 20 DAYS UNTIL TRIAL

Amina: Hey Holly, I know you probably don't want to hear from me right now.

But I wanted to let you know I really had no idea about that night at The Shack.

I hope you got home safe. I don't judge you by the way.

For choosing to deal with all of this the way you're choosing to.

Maybe there really aren't any right or wrong answers to this.

I hope you're okay. Let me know you got this?

Holly: Error Message 2083: The recipient you are sending to has chosen not to receive messages.

SOMETHING DIFFERENT (AGAIN)

Talia and I are getting together to get our hair done tonight.
I told her I wanted to do something different, when really,
I need a distraction from this trial being eighteen days away.

When Talia picks me up,
she says,

"You know, Mina, I understand the fashion switch up,
because you and I both know I've been in support of that for years—"

She laughs,
and I do in my head too,
but still manage to shoot her a side-eye that says:

Watch your mouth.

She continues,

"But I don't understand the switch up with your hair.
You used to say your 'fro was always a part of you.
What changed?"

IT'S SILLY, I KNOW.

I always saw girls who could change
their hair, clothes, and nails as the prototype.
Like the girls you're supposed to look like.

Girls like Talia.

Maybe this is my lesson in vulnerability.
Because I've never spoken about this before.

Who wants to admit they were jealous of a friend?

I tell Talia the truth anyway. These days,
I've learned sometimes telling the truth is hard,
but most times, when you tell it,
you have more to gain than lose.

"I always saw girls like you and girls on TV
and kind of believed that was the type of girl
I was supposed to look like."

LEARNING LESSONS, TOGETHER

I guess Talia and I are both learning lessons today,
because when I tell her how I've been feeling,
she says,

"I'm the one who was actually a little bit jealous of *you*."

I never thought Talia would ever have any reason to be jealous of me.
She's the one I have always believed had it made.
Loving family,
the car,
the clothes,
the looks.
Talia says:

"You taught me I don't have to be comfortable
when someone hits on me or tries to touch me on the bus.
You taught me it's all right to speak and say something.
Before you, I didn't really know what that looked like."

Our friendship hasn't been perfect,
but the thing about best friends is they never are,
and you love them in spite of it.

BACK AT THE SALON

"What are we doing with our hair today?"

are the first words I hear when we walk into Talia's aunt's salon.

The person I am now isn't the same.
But there are parts of me that I no longer want to change.
Parts of me that shouldn't change.

"I want the coils back,"

I say to Talia's aunt.

"But with a touch up on the highlights please."

Because some changes ain't half bad.

JULY 30: 13 DAYS UNTIL TRIAL

BEEF WITH WHOEVER WROTE THE BOOK™

Sundays at home have gotten even more unbearable.

Maybe it's the knowledge that before my life changed,
I'd never stay home on a Sunday.

Every week I've been home,
I've studied Bible stories from when I was younger
and every week,
I have a new beef with whoever wrote this book.

In the Bible, Mary's man didn't believe her.

I wonder if during this trial
if God will tell the people
the truth about who their pastor is,
or if I will have to bear the weight
of setting my own truth free.

QUESTION FOR DR. MILLER

"Dr. Miller, how do you deal with feeling
like you were in a situation you could have prevented?"

She asks me what I mean
and I grab my new journal and pen:

August 1

How do you stop getting so down on yourself? Sometimes I wonder if I didn't accept the job with Johnson, or if I told him I needed to go home that night instead of agreeing to go with him to the church, if any of this would have happened.

I've read all the pamphlets, and all the articles I can get my hands on. But sometimes I think I wouldn't have to do all this work, all this research, if I wasn't in this mess.

All the articles say what happened to you isn't your fault. But lately, I've been thinking about all the what-ifs and I've been struggling to understand.

KNOWING VS. BELIEVING

After I share with Dr. Miller what I've journaled,
she responds,
still looking at the corner of the room
before choosing her words,

"Well, I can tell you one thing.
You start by *believing* none of it was your fault.
Not just knowing, but believing it.
When's the last time you told yourself that
and believed it, Amina?"

I consider Dr. Miller's question, realizing,

"I don't know if I ever have."

NOT MY RESPONSIBILITY

Dr. Miller says:

That's the thing.
You cannot continue to try to understand
the mind of that man. He presented himself in a way
that forced his entire community to love him.

Abusers are master manipulators.
Sick people do sick things.
Your responsibility is not to understand him.

You do not understand the mind of an abuser,
because you are not sick like one.

AUGUST 5: 7 DAYS UNTIL TRIAL

THIS MORNING HOLLY TEXTS ME

for the first time since she's blocked me.

Holly: Hey Amina, I know it's been a while

and you probably don't want to talk to me anymore,

but if you do maybe we can meet and talk one more time?

Lately I've been trying to accept things out of my control.
I've been lucky to have a best friend
and boyfriend who are willing to forgive,
and my relationship with my father has been improving.

But the one thing I still have trouble accepting
is what went down with Holly.

So when Holly asks to talk,
I assumed I would be happy.
But somehow, all I can remember
is how hurt she was when we last spoke.

Amina: Hey Holly

Nice to hear from you for real, let's meet this Friday?

AUGUST 9: 3 DAYS UNTIL TRIAL

MEET ME AT THE PARK

Holly and I agreed to meet at the park by my house.

When we see each other,
it's as if we are meeting for the first time.

Like two people who know nothing about each other.
But the truth is,
we know more about each other than we've ever imagined.

HOLLY'S TURN

I ask Holly how she's doing
& she's quiet for a moment
before she finally says,

"I didn't come here to catch up, Amina.
I came here because I'm finally ready to talk to you.
I'm ready to tell you what I should have already said."

HOLLY'S RIGHT

Holly says,
"When I first reached out to you,
the least you could have done was respond."

I say,
"I'm—"

"And every single time,
every call,
every text,
every time I tried to talk to you,
you just treated me like I didn't exist."

I say,
"I'm so—"

"And then when you kept texting me,
it made me angry.
I reached out so many times to you.
Even before all of this,
I reached out wanting nothing more than to be a friend."

"Holly, I'm sorr—"

"And then after you learned that I was the girl who reported,
I was worth talking to again.
I don't think you really understand how that made me feel."

Holly's words hit my body sharper than a blade
because she's *right*.

I WAS WRONG

I tell Holly I'm sorry.
That I should have never treated her the way I did.
That I was wrong, and she deserved better.

She nods.
I'm not expecting her to accept my apology,
& to be honest, I wonder if I even deserve forgiveness.

Holly's right.
She's never done anything to me,
other than try to be a friend & instead of seeing that,
I saw only the parts of her that I resented.

I tell Holly if she's willing,
I'd like to be the friend to her that I should have been.

Holly doesn't say yes or no,
but she hugs me.

& it feels like I'm hugging a new,
yet somehow old,
friend.

PLAYING CATCH UP

Holly and I spend the next couple hours
catching up on her new (huge) house,
drama from my school,
and laughing about all the little shit in between.

She says she's finally getting adjusted to her new school,
and while nobody there knows about her or Johnson,
some parts of her still wish she'd stayed at Springfield High.

I ask her,

"You miss Springfield High for classes, the food, or the racism?"

And we laugh for the first time since we've seen each other.

Holly asks,

"Do you still have beef with that guy?
I think his name is B—"

I complete Holly's sentence,

"Bowl Cut. His name is Bowl Cut.
And yes, yes I do.
But that shouldn't come as a surprise to anyone."

Holly says,

"He always did kind of have his nose in everyone's business, huh?"

And this is the moment I know,
Holly and I may have more similarities than differences,
after all.

SHE SURVIVED

After an hour, Holly says
she has to go so she can beat the traffic going back home.

Holly says,

"I know the trial is coming up.
And I'm sorry I couldn't fight with you."

I've learned a lot about apologies these last few months.
I've been having to make a lot of them lately,
and one thing I've learned is every once in a while,
we apologize for things we shouldn't have to.

I tell her,

"You shouldn't be apologizing."

If I've learned one thing,
if I know anything at all,
it's that sometimes the fight
doesn't look the way we think it will.

Holly did fight. She fought,
because she survived.

AUGUST 12: TRIAL (DAY 1)

TODAY IS THE DAY

Today, on the first day of the trial,
my father drives nervously, tapping the steering wheel.

When we arrive in the courtroom,
it looks exactly the way you see on TV—except smaller
and the atmosphere feels much more daunting,
with a few journalists scattered throughout.

The room is split into two crowds.
My side consists of
my father,
Talia,
and a few ex-members of Holy Tabernacle.

Johnson's side outnumbers mine when it comes to number of bodies—
church folk,
community members,
his family.

Except for Deon, who sits on my side of the room—
right beside a woman I have only seen in photos he's shown.
His mother.
Her eyes offer an apology I wish her mouth did.

Last week, Deon told me that his mom had a change of heart.
That she was originally going to skip the trial,
because it would be too painful for her to see Johnson take the stand
but after speaking with Deon,
decided that if I was okay with it, she would go after all.
In support of me.

I check my phone to double-check it's silenced
& see a message from Talia:

Talia: Meet outside the courtroom real quick?

TALIA MEETS ME

with no words. Just the world's biggest
and best-timed hug.

Talia and I have spent our entire friendship
showing up and showing out for each other.

Our sisterhood's origin story
began in our pre-K classroom
when I opened my backpack to find my crayons
and a Bowl-Shaped Haircut Kid named Bryan
hollered about a big fat roach
crawling out from my backpack—

"Mina's dirty! She got roaches!"

and a girl named Natalia Luz Arias responded—

"Shut your ugly mouth!"

Before he tried to come for Talia,
I responded by stomping on the roach
and smearing the bottom of my shoe
all over his white sneakers until the dead roach stained.

Honestly, it's whatever Bowl Cut (and whoever dressed him) gets.
Who the fuck dresses a four-year-old in white sneakers?

When my teacher asked to speak to only me in the hall
Talia yelled:

"Stupid Big-Headed Bryan started it!"

After refusing to apologize to Bowl Cut,
Talia and I *both* got phone calls home.

After school Talia told me how she used to have roaches too.
Talia was the first person I ever invited to my house
(because Bowl Cut was right, we did have roaches),
and from that day on
a sisterhood was born.

We still have a sisterhood
worth stomping on, cursing out
any roach, pastor, or motherfucker
who tries either one of us.

STATE YOUR NAME FOR THE RECORD

I am asked to state my name and spell it for the record:

"Amina. A-M-I-N-A. Conteh. C-O-N-T-E . . ."

I glance over at Johnson
and I choke on the last letter,

". . . H."

The judge asks,

"Can you identify the defendant in the room?"

If I'm going to have to take a stand,
by way of the stand,
if I'm going to testify against my abuser,
share the one truth he may deny,
but we both know to be true,
I will look him in the eye.
Say,

"Yes, I see him."

Even with my voice breaking,
I am strong enough to look him in his face,
and say:

"His name is Randall Johnson."

AS MUCH AS I TRY TO FORGET HIM

I always know his name.

"Preacher."
"Community Figure."
But in this courtroom, he is
"RJ."
"Accused."
But still—
"Innocent Until Proven Guilty."
My father watches as a member of the courtroom,
bracing himself to hear the fate of the man he once called
"Friend."

Often, I catch myself
daydreaming of ways to seek revenge on him.
Perhaps shooting him—
drowning him in his own semen—
burning his home—
mimic the way he burned the home inside of me.
Mimic the way my father burned
on the inside.

The night I told him,
our living room filled with smoke.

I settle for time in this courtroom.
Marvel at its eeriness,
try concentrating on my breathing, but the air is thick here,
as if the presence of untold truths fills the room to capacity.

My stomach begins to feel as weak as an abuser's apology.

I convince myself this is just a conversation,
a spirited debate.
I am only answering questions everyone *thinks*
they know the answer to.

The first few questions are the easiest.

"What is your date of birth?"

"What school do you attend?"

"What is your current city of residence?"

and even those questions make my heart jump right out my chest
and into the middle of this courtroom.

TESTIFYING AGAINST YOUR ABUSER

is a lot like a Sunday morning service.

The audience is a congregation
ready for a word.

The judge and the jury
are Jesus and his disciples
waiting to hear all our sins.

And Johnson
is at an altar begging for forgiveness.

For survivors, the courtroom is meant to be
a place of justice
a sanctuary of healing
an opportunity to take back what the defendant stole.

Testifying is like saying your most desperate prayer
on a night when everyone in the world—or the courtroom
can hear you.

I am asked to recall the night of December 19.

On this judgment day
I open my mouth and testify to everything that
has tried to end me.
Everything that tried to silence me.
Everything that has tried to make a mess of my body:

ALL I REMEMBER (UNCENSORED)

Last December at the church, numbness made a home of my heart. Truth is, some days I wonder if Johnson tried to take more than my body. Some days, I still cannot recognize the body that belongs to **me**. Some days, I am consumed by everything I think I should have done differently:

I should have said "no" louder.

I should have never wanted the money.

I should have never gone with him to his office.

Truth is, I remember that night in   fragments.

I remember feeling as if life and time weren't real.

I remember feeling like I wanted to say everything—

but not being able to say anything.

And when it was finally over,

I remember feeling nothing at all.

Some nights, I still wear regret like a church dress. Wear guilt like some matching shoes **too**. Still think of how I should have been big enough to save myself,

                    instead of shrinking whisper small.

Still think the blame belongs to me

as if Johnson isn't the thief who attempted to steal

my voice   my joy   my pride   and the one thing that's
never waivered in my life—

my rage.

AUGUST 13: TRIAL (DAY 2)

I WAS PREPARED

My attorney said to prepare for Johnson's attorney
to argue it never happened.

I was prepared for that.

What I could never prepare myself for
was Johnson's wack-ass suit.

Metallic gray and probably purchased using
the tithes of one of my ex-church members.

Half of Johnson's supports are no longer
here after yesterday's testimony but

he still smooths his sleeves—treating the courtroom
like the same tired show he made of Sunday morning.

His clothing, almost as loud as his ego,
preparing himself to deny all that I—and he—knows to be true.

WHEN JOHNSON TAKES THE STAND

he treats the courtroom
as if the pulpit—or the podium—belongs to him.

His demeanor, laced with more confidence than mine
His voice, never wavering like mine.

He shares his testimony with as much conviction
as he does his sermons.

Tears fall—both his
and mine—as he tries to rewrite my story.

As heavy as this moment is for me—in some ways,
I feel like I've found the missing piece of a puzzle.

MISSING PIECE

These past few months,
I've been struggling to convince myself it wasn't my fault.

My mind had a way of convincing me,
it happened because I had

too much lip

too much sass

too much body

My mind had a way of convincing me,

it happened because I had

not enough lip

not enough sass

not enough body

Hearing Johnson share his testimony—his lie—
makes it clear to me,
what happened was *never* my fault.

What happened will always be the fault of the man,
who proclaims a lie so boldly, he convinces himself it's the truth.

What happened will always be the fault
of a man who had

too much power

too much ego

too much pride

What happened is the fault of the man

who should have *known better*.

who should have *lived better*.

The night of December 19
will always be the fault of the monster of a man known as

Randall Johnson.

AUGUST 14: TRIAL (DAY 3)

THE SCARIEST POSSIBILITY

Everyone has already warned me about the possibility
of Johnson being found not guilty.

These days, everyone expects me to prepare for the worst.

I know hearing a guilty verdict is not everything,
but I'd be lying if I said it's not something I hoped for.

IF I COULD REWRITE IT

Church folk will tell you,
Every trial in this life is meant to make you stronger,
like every tribulation is a personal improvement plan,
written & gifted by God.

I'm not sure how much I believe that to be true.

Truth is, if I could rewrite this story
I would change how I treated my friends.
Talia, Deon, & Holly.

I would change how I treated my father,
the anger I held toward him.

I would change how I treated myself,
knowing I was deserving of understanding and care.

If I could go back in time
& rewrite my story,
I would write Johnson right out of it.

Today,
I know that I'll never be able to rewrite those parts of me.

But I also know
that I have a village of people willing to fight with me
even through the parts of my story
I always thought nobody would read.

I am stronger.

Never because of Johnson
& what he put us through.
I am stronger,

in spite of Johnson
& what he put us through.

THE JURY HAS MADE A DECISION

On the final day of the trial,
the jury reaches a decision,
after a one-hour deliberation.

VERDICT

"We the jury,

find the defendant,

Randall Johnson,

Guilty."

GUILTY.

There's a sense of relief I feel
when I hear that word in the courtroom.

We find the defendant, Randall Johnson,
guilty.

Followed by the sting,
after I realize that many survivors don't.

On this day, I rose above.
Not because a jury believed me.
But because I did.

I spoke up.

Without blaming myself.
Ignoring the regrets and shame.

I stood firm in my truth.

The only truth.

BREAKING: Baltimore City Pastor Randall Johnson Convicted for Sexual Assault of a Minor

BALTIMORE, MD—Randall Johnson, 41, of Baltimore City, was found guilty by a jury of a sex crime involving a minor and former member of Holy Tabernacle AC, according to a release from the Baltimore City Prosecutor's Office.

Baltimore City Detective Katie Walbrook said Johnson frequently surrounded himself with the youth throughout Baltimore City, often serving as a mentor, confidant, and supervisor to many children between 12 and 17 years old. Johnson worked with these children at various events and activities, including outings and community outreach events, often promising monetary compensation to minors for work opportunities.

The sentencing is scheduled for September 27. Johnson faces up to 20 years in prison.

During his trial, the prosecutors presented evidence and testimony that the offense against the 16-year-old minor took place in Baltimore City in December of last year.

The Baltimore City Prosecutor's Office requests anyone with information to contact the Baltimore City Office Sex Crimes/Child Abuse Unit at (410) 555-2830.

Information can also be provided through the Baltimore City Crime Stoppers' Tip Line at 1-888-555-8423. All anonymous tips will be kept confidential.

AUGUST 15

AFTER THE VERDICT

my father doesn't speak much,
but he manages to say,

"I am *so* proud of you."

I believe him.

When we drive home,
we don't listen to the radio or gospel CDs.

But the silence isn't intimidating, or scary, or awkward.
It's like the quiet after a storm.

The last year made a whirlwind of our lives.
Wind blowing, waves crashing,
and we lived to tell the imperfect tale.

Today, the silence feels like another way of saying,

We survived.

THE LETTER

When my father and I get home,
he hands me a letter.

"I wrote this for you this morning."

August 15

When I say I am proud of you, I mean it every single time. Whether he is proven guilty in the eyes of the law or not. I wrote you this letter the morning before his verdict so you will know it to be true.

I am not the best with my words, I'm not the one with the quick tongue. That was your mother. But you have grown in ways that have carried that legacy in a way that I'm sure even she wouldn't have imagined. You persisted. Even when you didn't think you could.

This has not been an easy year. I have watched you grow, all from a situation we thought could only exist in nightmares.

I am so proud of you. For demanding attention in every room you walk in. For taking a stand. For being the daughter who gives me the privilege of being your father. And I am grateful that you chose to forgive me, even when I did not act as such.

I will love you for the rest of my days.

Love,

Dad

ALREADY WON

At my door, my father stands.
He does not know how to react to most things.
He processes his emotions slowly,
but today he is quick to respond.

"You know, your mom used to write letters
in the journal she had.
I noticed that you've been doing the same.
I thought, maybe I could write you something too."

He smiles,
walks over to me to give me a hug,
before he finally says,

"You found your way to fight back.
Even before today,
you won."

3 DAYS AFTER THE VERDICT

Holly: Hey Amina, congratulations on a guilty verdict.

I know it's been a while since we've spoken

but I want you to know I'm proud of you for taking this step.

Are you free for a phone call right now?

I have an idea and I'd love to talk about it with you.

PHONE CALL WITH HOLLY:

Holly: Hey, Amina, I thought

about what you said,

and I've found how I want to fight this.

> **Amina:** Hey, Holly, I'm all ears.
>
> Thanks for checking in by the way!

Holly: No, thank you, Amina.

Like you said.

We owe it to ourselves to heal.

Here's what I'm thinking . . .

54 DAYS AFTER THE VERDICT

SURVIVOR SPEAK-OUT

Holly suggested we plan a survivor speak-out circle.
In her words,

"There are so many ways to use your voice.
Johnson abused his to manipulate his community.
Why not use ours to heal our community?"

Holly and I spent two months
at the community center planning the event.

One thing I have learned from Dr. Miller
is some things really are easier to write down than say out loud.
So my guidance counselors helped us provide
a notepad and pen at the door for anyone who chose to write
rather than speak.

Holly spoke first.
It's the first time she's publicly shared her story
and even with her trembling voice,
the room grew still and clung to her every word.

I spoke next.
If you were to ask me a year ago
if I would be in front of a packed room of people sharing my story,
I wouldn't believe you,
but here I am doing just that.

Then Ms. Hamilton speaks.
Earlier she told me to listen for a special message,
but I didn't imagine she would say what I'm hearing.

Ms. Hamilton says when I spoke up about what happened to me,
it inspired her to address her own childhood trauma
and now she's looking for her own therapist.

It's amazing how you can inspire someone
in your lowest moments without even knowing it.

WHAT PEOPLE DON'T REALIZE

What people don't realize about rape
is you always feel as if everything is your fault.
You feel guilty for wasting the time of the jury—
as if you're taking away a biweekly paycheck.

Guilty for breaking the hearts of your loved ones—
as if you asked for all this to happen.

Guilty for destroying the assaulter's life—
as if your life hasn't changed forever.

But what I've come to realize is even on my worst days,
the fault is never mine to carry.

Even when I find myself taking one step forward,
and two steps back,
I can take pride in the fact that I have no blame to bear.

To start the event,
I suggest everyone take ten minutes to write down
how it is they are feeling in this very moment.

I write:

Testimonial

Every trial reaps a testimony

Ask me if I know of victory

I'll tell you

Witness this body and

Behold a miracle

Behold this narrative

Witness a masterpiece

After

    A

            Wreckage.

AUTHOR'S NOTE

All the Fighting Parts is first and foremost a hug to survivors like my younger self. Secondly, it's my way of calling out abusers and organizations who protect them.

My abuser, like Pastor Johnson, was well liked within my former church community. Speaking out against him felt impossible. I spent many years blaming myself for what happened to me. I had thoughts like *If I didn't wear that dress*, or *If I didn't choose to go there*, or *If I didn't trust them*.

It wasn't until writing Amina's story—the story of a girl who is messy and flawed—that I truly learned that, as survivors, the shame we experience surrounding our assault is not ours to carry. It never was.

I hope you feel empowered by Amina's story. I hope you know that even on the difficult days, you are still a fighter.

RESOURCES

ME TOO: The "me too." movement supports survivors of sexual violence and their allies by connecting survivors to resources, offering community organizing resources, pursuing a "me too." policy platform, and working with researchers to add to the field and chart the way forward. Learn more at Metoomvmt.org.

RAINN: RAINN (Rape, Abuse & Incest National Network) is the nation's largest anti–sexual violence organization. RAINN created and operates the National Sexual Assault Hotline in partnership with more than one thousand local sexual assault service providers across the country and operates the DoD Safe Helpline for the Department of Defense. RAINN also carries out programs to prevent sexual violence, help survivors, and ensure that perpetrators are brought to justice. Learn more at Rainn.org.

TURNAROUND: Turn Around's mission is to educate, empower, and advocate for all people impacted by intimate partner violence, sexual violence, and human trafficking. Learn more at Turnaroundinc.org.

ACKNOWLEDGMENTS

To my family, Ethleen, Andrena, and Mom, thank you for fighting with me. I love you.

To Sis. Cheryl Bryant, I cannot thank you enough for protecting us and speaking up so fiercely. I love you. I know you're throwing the best red shoe party in heaven!

To my Pitch Wars mentors Dante Medema and Liz Lawson, thank you for seeing something in my manuscript even when it was giving MESS! You were a light during a dark time. #TEAMNEMESIS!

Joy McCullough, thank you for your unwavering support, your work, and your story. You gave me courage to share mine.

Elizabeth Acevedo, thank you for your kind words and thoughtful advice. Thank you for telling me to "Write the damn book!" I WROTE THE DAMN BOOK!

Jordan Hill and Joanna Volpe, thank you for picking my novel out from the slush. Thank you for championing it and finding it such a wonderful home. Thank you for giving Amina a microphone!

Maggie Lehrman and Emily Daluga, it means so much to me to work with editors who prioritized the integrity of Amina's voice while also challenging me to make the story better. I'm forever grateful.

Rachelle Baker and Micah Fleming, the artist and designer for the stunning cover of this book, thank you for capturing Amina so beautifully!

To the good folks at Abrams: Amy Vreeland, Maggie Moore, Mary Marolla, Megan Evans, Kristen Luby, Kim Lauber, Hallie Patterson, Elisa Gonzales, and Andrew Smith, thank you for giving this story a loving home. Thank you for your support!

To my sister-friend, Beth, we've been through hell and back. We won. I love you down, girl!

To my DewMore family, Sadiyah, Mohamed, Mecca, Derick, Brion, Chakra, and Slang, thank you for helping me find my power. For providing me a safe space to be angry, (and encouraging me to use my voice to do something about it.) "B-MORE POETS, COULDN'T BE MORE POET!" Special shout-out to Kenneth, the first person I spoke to about this novel. I love you!

To my ACT-SO family, thank you for the safe space you provide for young people and for helping hone my poetic voice. Teenage Hann could always count on laughs and love every Tuesday. Always a proud alumna. #IThinkSoThereforeIACTSO!

To my Pitch Wars friends, Xan, Alli, Gabrielle, Juliet, Hetal, and Tia, I'm so grateful to have met you. Our zoom sprints (featuring the wineglass damn near the size of my head!) were a highlight of the shitshow that was 2020. Maria, I'm so thankful for our writing sprints, and your kind heart. Forever grateful you're in my life. Sara, thank you for our FaceTime calls, chaotic texts, and for being a beautiful friend to me.

To the 2023 debuts, WE DID IT! Special shoutout to Brittany, Kaylie, Jade, Page, and Danielle!

To the Shaw family, thank you for your kindness. Destiny and Obria, thank you for supporting me so fiercely when [redacted] happened. LOL.

To my Morgan homies, Saudah, Maya, Justin, Kardel, Lowe Key, and Ki, we got memories for DAYS. I cherish them all. A. J. Verdelle, thank you for believing in me enough to encourage and work with me. Thank you for challenging me.

To my New School homies, Crysta, Stone, Gabrielle, and Jon, I'm thankful to have gone through grad school with your friendship. Forever grateful to my professors as well, especially Camille Rankine and Robert Polito!

Finally, my father, thank you for listening to me. Whether it's 2 p.m. or 2 a.m. The summer I reported, you told me, "You will have the last word." I didn't believe it then but know it now. Thank you for supporting me. We've come so far. I got you, always. "Your pain is my pain, and your fight is my fight." Forever. I love you.